JAILBAIT

Lesléa Newman

delacorte press

Published by Delacorte Press
an imprint of Random House Children's Books
a division of Random House, Inc.
New York

www.randomhouse.com/teens

Educators and librarians, for a variety of teaching tools, visit us at
www.randomhouse.com/teachers

The Library of Congress has cataloged the hardcover edition of this work as follows:

Newman, Lesléa.
Jailbait / Lesléa Newman.
p. cm.
Summary: In 1971, unpopular and lonely tenth-grader Andi—teased at her Long Island
high school for her large breasts and ignored at home by her distant parents—builds a
fantasy romantic life around her clandestine, sexual relationship with a man in his thirties.
ISBN-13: 978-0-385-73198-0 (trade) — ISBN-13: 978-0-385-90230-4 (glb)
ISBN-10: 0-385-73198-1 (trade) — ISBN-10: 0-385-90230-1 (glb)
[1. Sex—Fiction. 2. Self-esteem—Fiction. 3. Emotional problems—Fiction.
4. Parent and child—Fiction. 5. High schools—Fiction. 6. Long Island (N.Y.)—Fiction.
7. Schools—Fiction.] I. Title.

PZ7.L47988Jai 2005
[Fic]—dc22
2004009559
ISBN-13: 978-0-385-73405-9 (tr pbk)
ISBN-10: 0-385-73405-0 (tr pbk)

The text of this book is set in 12.5-point Apollo.

Book design by Angela Carlino

Printed in the United States of America

December 2006

10 9 8 7 6 5 4 3 2 1

First Trade Paperback Edition

For A.F.
older and wiser

jailbait (jal/bat/) n. *Slang.* 1. a girl with whom sexual intercourse is punishable as statutory rape because of her youth. 2. a sexually attractive young girl. 3. any temptation to commit a crime punishable by imprisonment. (JAIL + BAIT)

—*Webster's Encyclopedic Unabridged Dictionary*

NY Penal Code §130.25 [2] (as it read in 1971)
A male is guilty of rape in the third degree when: Being twenty-one years old or more, he engages in sexual intercourse with a female less than seventeen years old.

"Oh, please. There's no such thing as statutory rape. That girl knew exactly what she was doing."

—*anonymous woman (overheard in a coffee shop)*

Prologue

Greenwood. What a stupid name. First of all, wood is brown, not green, and second of all, who makes up these dumb names, anyway? Like Flatbush, where my grandmother used to live before she moved to Florida. Have you ever seen a flat bush? Me neither.

If they had asked me, I would have called this town Boresville. It's not even a town, really, it's a suburb with a million boring houses that look just like ours. A kitchen, living room, and dining room downstairs, and three bedrooms upstairs: one for me; one for my Parental Units, Shirley and Fred; and one for my brother, Mike, who's seven years older than me, only he's away at college.

When I was little, I thought college was a place, you know, like New Jersey. Everyone was always saying, "My brother went to college." "My sister's in college." So I figured college was a faraway place they ship you off to when you reach a certain age. Which they sort of do, really, only college isn't one place, it's a lot of places like Princeton, Harvard, and Yale. Only in Mike's case it's SUNY Buffalo and with his grades he's lucky he even got to go there. It's his third college because he keeps dropping out and going back, but it's not like Mike's brain-dead or anything. He just doesn't care. And neither do I. I mean, everyone knows how useless school is. Take geography, for example. Can somebody please give me one good reason why I have to know that the largest state in the country is Alaska? If there ever actually comes a time in my life when I need to know this vital information, I'll just look it up in the encyclopedia.

Anyway, I don't worry about my grades much because I don't even want to go to college. But I would never tell Shirley or Fred that. They would just *kill* me. I still remember the big fight Fred and Mike had the day Mike told the Units he didn't want to go. All Mike wanted to do was get an apartment with some friends in the city, take a year off, and just *live* a little. You'd think he wanted to shave his head, pierce his nose, and join the Jews for Jesus the way Fred blew his stack about it. "I didn't work my butt off all these years so some lousy kid of mine would wind up living on the street selling used books in front of Cooper Union," he yelled so loud his glasses steamed up and his face turned red.

I don't see what the big deal is. Shirley never went to college. She married Fred right after she graduated from high school and then worked in a stationery store—now there's an exciting career—while Fred went to college and med school and then became a dentist. Then she had Mike and then she had me and then when I was two, we all moved from Manhattan to Greenwood to live happily ever after. Yeah, right. I can't wait until I'm old enough to get out of here. I want to move to a really hip city like San Francisco and live in a totally cool apartment with a bunch of friends who are all writers and musicians and artists and stuff, and we'll all be really famous, only I'm not good at anything so I have no idea what I'll be famous for yet.

In the meantime, though, I'm stuck here in Boresville. For three more years. Fred and Shirley won't even let me go into the city and walk around Greenwich Village by myself even though it's only an hour and twenty minutes away on the train. They used to say, "When you're sixteen," and now that I'm almost sixteen, they say, "When you're seventeen." Fred and Shirley moved us out to Long Island—at least that name makes sense, it *is* a long island—because they both grew up in New York City, which they think is the most disgusting, dirty, dangerous place on the planet, as opposed to the suburbs, which are so serene, sanitary, and safe.

Ha. If they only knew.

ONE

So this is how it started: It's September 7, 1971, the first day of tenth grade, and I'm walking home after school because I hate taking the bus. No, cancel that. I *refuse* to take the bus because something always happens on it that makes me look like an idiot. Either Donald Caruso, this junior who just lives to make my life miserable, will stick his big ugly foot out in the aisle to trip me and then laugh his head off like that's the funniest thing in the world, or Hillary Jacoby, who is so desperate to be popular she picks on the lowest of the low (me), will accidentally-on-purpose smush a wad of Bazooka bubble gum into my hair and then look around to see if anyone is impressed with how clever she is.

But that's just kid stuff compared to what happened on a certain day last spring when I woke up late and almost missed the bus. The bus driver saw me running in his rearview mirror and slammed on his brakes so I could catch up. Now, I'm not a person who runs very often, and I guess things were flapping in the breeze because as soon as I climbed on board, before I even had a chance to catch my breath, the whole bus burst into song:

"Do your boobs hang low?
Do they wobble to and fro?
Can you tie 'em in a knot?
Can you tie 'em in a bow?
Can you throw 'em over your shoulder
Like a continental soldier?
Do your boobs hang low?"

I crossed my arms over my more than ample chest, turned around, and pushed against the door until the bus driver opened it. Then I ran off the bus and swore that from that day on, even if it was raining or snowing or bright purple UFOs were falling from the sky, I would never set foot on a school bus again.

So like I said, I'm walking home from school, down Farm Hill Road, with my army green knapsack on my back, just minding my own business, when this car goes by. Usually I don't notice cars—I mean, a car is a car is a car as far as I'm concerned, unlike Fred, who thinks cars are so important he has to trade in his Caddie every year for a more up-to-date model even though I can never tell the difference.

But this car is really, well, *cute,* which is a funny way to describe a car, but it is. It's a brown Volkswagen Bug, and you don't see too many of those driving around Suffolk County—also known as Suffocation County—let me tell you. The only other Volkswagen I've ever seen was an orange VW hippie van that belonged to Kevin, this friend of Mike's. Kevin came to pick Mike up one day, and Fred took one look out the window and started screaming, "No kid of mine is getting into a car made by those lousy Krauts," and then Mike screamed back, "Simmer, Freddie—boy, I wasn't even born yet," meaning World War II and everything, and then Fred screamed even louder, "Don't get fresh with me, Michael Kaplan. You'll get into that car over my dead body," which made me think, *That could be arranged, Daddy-o,* but not really, of course.

So anyway, Kevin drove off, and two seconds later Mike said he was going for a walk, and you'd have to be a total retard not to figure out that he was meeting Kevin on the corner. Anyway, the point is, since we're Jewish and my father grew up during the Holocaust, he is absolutely psycho about the Germans and World War II, he really is. He says Volkswagens are the perfect German car because the motor's in the back so if you get into a head-on collision, the SOBs can just haul your body out of the car and still use the engine. Fred is so anti-German he won't even let us eat sauerkraut on our hot dogs and I'm not even kidding.

So of course I notice the little brown Volkswagen. It looks like a cartoon almost, like a little Hershey's Kiss scooting around in the sun. It's funny when you think about it, but I had no idea then how that little car was going to change my life forever. I didn't think, for example, *Before you know it, Andi Kaplan, you're going to be sitting in that little brown Bug doing things you never even imagined*. Nope, the thought doesn't even cross my mind. I just stand there and watch the car for a minute, and then I walk over to the fence and call Bessie by clicking my tongue against my teeth.

Bessie's a cow, in case you're wondering. Believe it or not, there actually is a farm on Farm Hill Road, though there isn't any hill. Back in the old days, about a million years before we moved here, Long Island used to be just one big potato farm, which is kind of hard to believe since now it's all developments and grocery stores and gas stations and stuff. This farm on Farm Hill Road is pretty much the only farm left around here, and as far as I know, Bessie's the only cow. I don't even know if her name is really Bessie or not. I just call her that.

See, the Rents won't let me have a pet, so I pretend Bessie is mine. I've wanted a puppy ever since I could talk, but Shirley and Fred refuse to let me have one. First Shirley went on and on about how a dog would shed its smelly wet fur all over her precious living room furniture, which is really a lame excuse because all the chairs and couches are covered with plastic anyway. Then when I told her we could get a poodle, since poodles don't shed at all, she started in on how it would track mud all over her precious shag carpeting, which is hard enough to keep clean as it is since I never remember to wipe my feet. Finally, when I didn't let up, the Rents said maybe I could get a pet when I was older, and now that I am older, Shirley's line is "You're going off to college in a few years. Who's going to take care of it then?" Like I would really go off to college and not take my pet.

I thought of asking someone to give me a puppy for my birthday last year so that Shirley and Fred would have to let me keep it. Like when I was twelve, the Units finally let me get my ears pierced for my birthday but they only let me wear posts, so I got my friend Ronnie to buy me a pair of gold hoops and then what could they say? Somehow, though, I don't think it would work with an animal. And besides, Ronnie moved to Pennsylvania last spring and I don't really have any other friends, but that's another story.

Anyway, at least I have Bessie. I started hanging out with her last spring when I stopped taking the bus and she's pretty used to me now. Even though I only saw her about once a week over the summer, she still remembers me. As soon as she sees me, she ambles over to the fence, which takes a while because Bessie doesn't do anything in a hurry. I don't know how old she is, but she walks like she's about a hundred and she's all bony besides. She's light brown, sort of a tawny color, except for the tip of her tail, which is black, and she's got the biggest, most beautiful eyes you've ever seen. They're dark, dark brown, like the gooey hot fudge they pour over your ice cream at Howard Johnson's, only Shirley never lets me order a sundae because she thinks I should do myself a favor and join Weight Watchers like she did. I don't have a big potbelly like Fred or anything but I'm not exactly skinny like Shirley either. I'm definitely soft and lumpy in certain places, not that I really care. But Shirley thinks it's never too early for a girl to start watching her figure, since it's never too early for the boys to start watching it. Yeah, right.

For your information, Shirley's going through the Change. Fred told me about it. He says it's a time in a woman's life when she really goes crazy. Great. Something else to look forward to. First Shirley dyed her hair blond—like that looks really natural—and then she got completely obsessed with her weight. After sitting on her butt for forty-nine years, she finally decided to join an exercise place for women called Elaine Powers Figure Salon, and now she practically lives there when she's not playing cards or going clothes shopping or eating lunch with her friends. Shirley was never really fat or even chubby like yours truly. She was just normal-sized before, but now she's about a size two because all she ever puts in her mouth are cigarettes and celery.

"Hey, Bessie, how's my sweet girl? Come say hi. C'mon, girl." I shrug off my knapsack and coax her over. When she finally gets to the fence, I pull up some grass and let her take it out of my hand.

"How's my best girl, huh, Bessie?" I ask her. She doesn't answer me, of course. But it doesn't matter. I know it sounds silly, but I feel like even though Bessie can't talk, she totally understands me. And it's a good thing too, since nobody else does.

I stand there for a while, petting Bessie and talking to

her. Bessie feels real soft like velvet if you run your hands the right way down her back, and rough like corduroy if you go the wrong way, which I never do. I tell her about my stupid, boring day at school, which is pretty much the same as every other stupid, boring day I've ever had to get through at school: math, science, English, social studies, French, gym, and of course Donald Caruso torturing me at lunch.

"Hey, where's your girlfriend?" he asked when he saw I was sitting by myself. "Oh, I forgot. Your girlfriend moved to Transylvania. You poor, poor thing. All alone in the world." Donald sniffled and pretended to wipe tears from his eyes, the big idiot. And not only that, he said *girlfriend* in this high, squeaky voice, like Ronnie and I were girlfriends in the boyfriend/girlfriend sense of the word. Which, for your information, we weren't.

I tried to just ignore him, but it's hard because Donald Caruso really gets on my nerves, even though every other girl in my class thinks he's God's gift to women. I don't know how his girlfriend stands him, I really don't. But in a way it makes sense because for some insane reason, Donna Rizzo is completely obsessed with frogs. She has a million frog stickers on her notebooks, she carries all her stuff in a frog backpack, and she wears this frog pin made of green rhinestones every single day. So of course she's in love with Donald Caruso, the ugly frog who she hopes will turn into a handsome prince someday. Though if I were her, I wouldn't hold my breath.

Anyway, I tell Bessie everything while she chews her

grass and listens. "How am I ever going to get through an entire school year, huh, Bessie?" I ask her. She has no idea, and neither do I.

✖ ✖ ✖

The next day the brown Volkswagen goes by again when I'm walking home from school, and it goes by again the day after that too. Finally on Friday when it drives by, the guy behind the wheel honks at me. It's a friendly honk, those two little beep-beeps you make by tapping the horn with the heel of your hand. Not a long obnoxious honk like this one time when I was walking home and this stupid businessman in a huge blue car slowed down, leaned on his horn, and yelled, "Hey, honey, nice headlights! Shine 'em over here!" Gross. But this is different; this is definitely a friendly honk, I can just tell. So I look up and wave and the guy waves back and then he drives off and I watch his car until it gets to the end of the road and turns left.

And that's it. Pretty exciting, huh? Believe it or not, it is. Which just goes to show you how totally boring life gets around here. A stranger in a brown car waves at me and I get butterflies in my stomach—how pathetic is that? Now I'll have to wait until Monday to see if he honks at me again. Bummer. Most kids would be glad it's Friday, but not me. Weekends are even more boring than weekdays, if that's even possible. There's nothing to do except maybe go shopping with Shirley, and believe me, there's nothing more boring than that.

"Hey, Bessie. Hi, pretty girl." I make my clicking noise and she comes over to the fence. "That guy waved at me, did you see that? You think he's my knight in shining armor and he's going to take me away from all this?"

Bessie looks startled, like her feelings are hurt.

"No offense," I say quickly, because I don't want her to think I want to be taken away from her pasture. I like hanging out with Bessie. When I stand here and pet her back like this, I feel, well, peaceful is the only way to describe it. Not like the rest of my life, where I feel like I'm suffocating and if something doesn't happen in two seconds I'm going to choke or throw up or do something that will make me even less popular than I already am.

And for your information, I'm not a total idiot; I know the chances of having a knight in shining armor come to rescue me are slim to none, but hey, it could happen. Why not? Ever hear of Romeo and Juliet? Strange as this may seem, I do believe in love at first sight. I'm sure you're surprised to hear that because I'm so negative about everything, but you know, most people are just the opposite of what they appear to be. Like clowns who are always trying to make people laugh? If you look really close, you can see how sad they are. And have you ever seen actors when they aren't acting? Like when they're on those afternoon talk shows Shirley always watches after her soap operas. Actors are actually the shyest people you can imagine. I know I come off as pretty tough, but underneath, I'm just a big mush ball.

"Stranger things have happened, right, Bess?" I ask. She chews her cud slowly, like she's thinking it over. I wonder why I'm never bored when I'm out here with Bessie, like I am every other minute of my life. Maybe it's because Bessie doesn't want anything from me like everyone else does: my teachers, who are always yelling at me to pay attention; Fred, who's forever screaming at me to take out the garbage, which is my job now that Mike's gone; and Shirley, who's constantly nagging me to do something with my hair so it isn't hanging in my eyes, or wear different, nicer clothing, or be a different, nicer person.

Or maybe I like hanging out with Bessie because I'm just plain weird. I'll give you twenty bucks if you can find a tenth grader at Greenwood High who'll argue with you about that. I'm not *weird* weird, like Marlene Pinkus, who wears nothing but pink—her pants, her sweaters, her shoes, her barrettes, even her socks and, though I can't say for sure, probably her underwear. Or Stephen Taubman, another bona fide wacko, who sits in front of me in science class, picks his nose constantly, and saves all his snot in this little metal box for God only knows what reason and I'm not even kidding. I'm just mildly weird, I guess. I'm not like most of the girls in my class, who are into boys and makeup and *Seventeen* magazine and stuff. And I'm not a jock because I throw like a girl, and I'm not a hippie chick because I think tie-dyed clothes are ugly, and I'm not artsy-fartsy like the kids who hang around the art room throwing blobs of clay around on the pottery wheel. My school is definitely full of cliques. I'm just a clique unto myself, I guess.

I hang out with Bessie a little while longer, not saying anything, not doing anything, not wanting anything. Then I take my big butt home.

TWO

It's Sunday night, and for some reason, because I'm bored out of my skull, I guess, or maybe because I'm hoping to see Mr. VW tomorrow, I decide to set my hair like Ronnie showed me one day a few years ago after I got called "frizz bomb" thirty times before first period even started. So after I take my shower, I gather all my hair up on top of my head in a high ponytail, wrap it around a big orange juice can, and pin the whole thing to the top of my head with a million bobby pins. Then, just as I'm trying to figure out how I'm going to sleep like this, Fred calls up the steps for me to come into the kitchen. I ignore him, but after he yells two more times, I put on my bathrobe and go downstairs.

"What's this?" Fred comes up right next to me and peers through the orange juice can on top of my head like it's a telescope. "Land ho! Thar she blows!" he says with a chuckle.

"Ha, ha. Very funny," I say, stepping away from him. "What do you want?"

"Your brother's on the phone," he says, gesturing with the top of his bald head toward Shirley, who's sitting at the kitchen table with the receiver pressed against her ear, finishing up her conversation.

"Call us next week and let us know how your classes are going. Oh, and Mike, let me know what color you're decorating your room, and measure the windows so I can send you and your roommate some curtains."

I can just see Mike rolling his eyes over that one.

"Okay, wait, here's your sister. Hang on." Shirley hands me the receiver.

"Hey, Mike."

"Hi, Squirt." Mike's called me Squirt ever since I was two seconds old. "How's life with the Eunuchs?"

"Far-out. Groovy. Outta sight," I say, in a tone that conveys just the opposite. "How's college?"

"Like high school with ashtrays," he answers. "And speaking of ashtrays . . . Mary Jane just got here. All right! Hang on a second, Squirt."

"Mary Jane? Mike, not again!" Mary Jane is Mike's code for pot. The smoking kind, not the cooking kind. I hear him say, "Hey, man, pass that doobie over here," and then someone must crank up his stereo, because all I hear after that is Jimi Hendrix singing "Purple Haze" so loud it's like he's wailing right in my ear. I play with the phone cord and say, "Yeah. Uh-huh," a few times so the Rents don't get suspicious, until Mike finally gets back on the line.

"Mike, don't you think you should hang out with Mary Jane a little less and study a little more?" I ask in a stage whisper. "Have you even gone to any classes yet?"

"Don't be so uptight, Squirt. Nobody goes to classes the first week."

"Mike"—I lower my voice even further—"Fred is going to have ten conniptions if you get kicked out again."

"Don't be such a drag, all right, Squirt? Hey, the brewski just arrived, I gotta split."

"Wait a second. Mike—" But before I can say anything else, he hangs up.

"Your brother sounds pretty good, doesn't he?" Shirley asks as I put the receiver back in its cradle on the wall. "I think he's going to do well this year. I think he's finally turned over a new leaf."

Yeah, right. The only leaf Mike's going to turn over is on a marijuana plant.

"Who's this Mary Jane?" Fred asks. "Didn't he have a girlfriend named Mary Jane last year?"

"Uh . . . " I pretend to think. "I don't remember."

"I bet she transferred to be with Mike up at Buffalo," Shirley says. "And who can blame her, really? Mike's a very good-looking guy."

"He'd be a lot better-looking if he cut off that pony-tail of his," Fred grumbles.

"Oh, you're just jealous," Shirley says with a laugh, nodding at Fred's shiny pink scalp.

"Jealous? That's a good one. You think I want to go around looking like a girl? I'd like to take a pair of scissors myself and—"

"Good night, Shirley. Good night, Fred." It's definitely time to make my great escape.

"Good night, Andrea." Shirley says, staring at my head. I know she's dying to say something about my hair, but always the queen of tact, she manages to restrain herself.

"Don't you want to watch *World of Disney* with us?" Fred asks.

"No thanks."

"How about a game of Monopoly?"

"No thanks."

"Chinese checkers?"

"I don't think so."

"Scrabble?"

"Fred, I'm really tired," I say, and then before he can make me another offer I just can't refuse, I turn and run up the stairs.

The next morning when I open my eyes, I'm lying on my back with the orange juice can all smushed to the side, even though I fell asleep on my stomach with my head hanging off the edge of my bed. And when I comb my hair out, it looks a little better than usual, except there's this bumpy ridge right next to my part that isn't exactly attractive. But it's too late to do anything about it, so I throw on some clothes and walk myself to school. And besides, who's going to notice my hair anyway?

Donald Caruso, that's who. The minute I open my locker, he catches sight of me. And he can't just say something nice, like "Andi, you look good today," which is what a civilized person would do, and leave it at that. No-o-o-o. He has to look me up and down with this stupid smirk on his face and say, "Hey Dee-Dee. I'm so *dee*-lighted to see you today. You look un-usually *dee*-vine."

This is how Donald Caruso busts my chops pretty much on a daily basis. Instead of calling me Andi, he calls me Dee-Dee in reference to my oversized knockers, which probably are a size D by now, though I wouldn't know since I haven't bought a new bra in over a year. And it's true, my 38C bras have gotten tight. I think of myself as more like a C-plus, which is how my teachers think of me too, at least according to my report card.

Anyway, I try to ignore Donald, but then of course he sticks his oversized sneaker in my way so I can't shut my locker.

"Hey, c'mon, Donald, I have to go," I say, but he doesn't move.

"No need to get *dee*-fensive, Dee-Dee. What's the big hurry?" he asks. "You have to go call your *girlfriend*?" He gestures toward the pay phone at the end of the hall and then clasps his hands to his chest, sighs, and puts this stupid moony look on his face. "Ah, young love."

"Oh, shut up," I say, and he answers, "Blow me," which is his all-time favorite expression. I swear, Donald Caruso has the intelligence of a gerbil, my apologies to the animal kingdom. Finally Donna shows up with an unusually ugly frog barrette holding back her hair, and off they go, his big hairy arm draped across her thin bony shoulder, and her little skinny arm looped around his thick wrestler's waist. I don't know how she stands him, I swear to God, I really don't. If I were her, I'd definitely have my head examined.

The rest of the day drags by, and when the last bell finally rings, it's not a moment too soon. I grab my jacket, slam my locker, and head out, right past all those lined-up yellow school buses that look like overgrown sticks of butter about to melt in the sun. I keep my pace steady because if I walk too slow, I might miss the guy in the Volkswagen altogether, and if I walk too fast, I'll just have to stand there like I'm waiting for him and wouldn't that look stupid? This whole thing is stupid; it's crazy, I don't even know the guy. But hey, maybe he'll be my friend or something, you never know. I certainly could use the company. And he's got to be more mature than the boys at school, which wouldn't take much, let me tell you. I swear, if one more boy blows into his elbow to make a farting noise when I walk by, I am going to just haul off and slug him. Especially if his name is Donald Caruso.

And speaking of the world's biggest jerk, I can't believe he noticed that I at least tried to look good today. Don't get me wrong, I'm not a total slob or anything. It's just that I don't think appearances are anything to get all hyped up about. Yeah, right. Just try telling that to the girls in my class and they'll look at you like your face just turned bright green like the Wicked Witch of the

West in *The Wizard of Oz* or something. I mean, you should see them all crammed together like sardines in the girls' room before first period, trying to get a spot in front of the mirror. The way they all push and shove, you'd think something really important was written over their reflections, like the name of the boy they're going to marry, which is all most of them care about anyway. I mean, they are *so* shallow. All anyone talked about today was who went to fat camp and lost weight over the summer, who got a nose job, who got their braces off, who got contact lenses, and what everybody was wearing. I of course wore the same thing I always do: a black sweater over a pair of dungarees, with black high-top sneakers.

Shirley tried to take me shopping for school clothes this year—she tries every year—but I refused to go. The last time we went shopping I practically lost my lunch at the way Shirley and the salesgirl were oohing and aahing over all the cashmere sweaters and pleated skirts I wouldn't be caught dead wearing.

"Isn't this adorable?" Shirley asked, holding up a belted red and green plaid jumper with a matching red sweater. When I didn't answer, a salesgirl who was standing nearby started cozying up to her.

"Oh that's a very popular outfit," the girl said, and the way Shirley turned around and started in on how they're wearing their skirts so short this year, and how you have to have really great legs to get away with that, and blah blah blah, I could just tell she wished more than anything that the salesgirl with her perfectly straight hair, her frosty pink lipstick and nails, and her color-coordinated skirt and sweater set were her daughter instead of me.

This year, Shirley waited until the second-to-last week in August before she started in on me about my "wardrobe," as she calls it. It was one of those days when it's so hot you wish you didn't have to wear your skin, let alone your clothing. She was drinking sugar-free iced tea in a tall Bugs Bunny glass that we got free from the gas station with our last fill-up and browsing through the JCPenney circular. "Isn't this dress cute?" she asked, pointing to a page. "Let's go shopping this afternoon. It's cool in the mall, and besides, you could use a few new outfits."

"Outfits" for God's sake. That just about killed me. I haven't worn an "outfit" since first grade.

"I have everything I need," I told her.

"Don't you want a few new dresses or skirts?" Shirley asked, like I had turned into someone else overnight. "I wish you would wear something colorful," she went on. "Why do you always have to wear black?"

Because I know it bugs you, I wanted to say, but of course I didn't. You'd think Shirley would be glad I always wear black, since according to *Redbook* and *Good Housekeeping* and all those other magazines she's always reading, black makes you look thinner. But it just goes to show you that when it comes to Shirley, I can't do anything right.

"Black is the presence of all colors," I said, quoting my art teacher, but Shirley wasn't impressed. She just started in on me about always wearing dungarees instead of skirts, but I refuse to wear anything else. I like dungarees because they have lots of pockets and I carry lots of stuff: my Swiss army knife in case I need to open a soda bottle or peel an orange, my keys, some money, and my lucky shell.

I got my lucky shell from Mike, who gave it to me one day when he was a senior and cut school, though of course I wasn't supposed to know that. Mike walked into the house with his shoes all sandy from the beach and said, "Now don't say I never gave you anything," and I said, "Oh, thanks a lot," like *My brother went to Jones Beach and all I got was this lousy shell,* but actually I was really surprised that in the middle of cutting school and hanging out with his friends and smoking dope, Mike thought of me. So I keep it in my pocket for luck.

I'm touching my shell right now, in fact, as I make my way over to Farm Hill Road, walking with my hands in my pockets and my head down as usual, but I feel on the alert like a dog with her ears perked up, waiting for the sound of her master's step. And then there it is, the putt-putt of the Volkswagen's engine, and before I can stop it, my right hand snakes its way out of my pocket and waves, and worse than that, this stupid smile breaks across my face like I just won a trip for two to Hawaii from Monty Hall on *Let's Make a Deal*. I feel like such an idiot, but luckily Mr. VW doesn't seem to notice. He toot-toots the horn like he did on Friday, gives a little wave, and keeps driving. I watch the car and I think I see him checking me out in the rearview mirror but I'm not sure. Anyway, I can't let him see that I'm checking him out while he's checking me out, so I look away and by the time I look back, all I can see is the tail end of his tailpipe and then the little Volkswagen is gone.

✖ ✖ ✖

Tuesday afternoon is all overcast and I'm praying, even though I'm not sure if I believe in God or not, *Please don't let it rain. Please don't let it rain.* I mean, I'd look really stupid standing out there soaking wet waiting for the brown Volkswagen to go by. Then again, maybe it should rain. Then maybe my guy would roll down his window and say, "Hey, kid, don't you know enough to come in out of the rain?" and give me a ride.

I walk down the road at my usual pace, with my back straight to improve my lousy posture. Shirley's always after me to stand up nice and tall because she thinks it makes me look thinner. Give me a break. What it really does is make my breasts stick out more. Which is a huge and I mean *huge* problem, but there's not much I can do about it. I don't want them sagging down to my waist or anything like my grandmother's. She has real hangers, let me tell you.

I guess I take after my grandmother in that department, because unlike the two of us, Shirley's pretty flat. Believe it or not, I started getting breasts when I was only in third grade. First they were small, though they were certainly big enough for the other kids to notice and tease me about. ("What are those, pimples on your chest?") They stayed that way for about a year and then one day they just started growing, and they grew and grew and grew and there was just no stopping them. I mean, I am definitely what you call stacked. Which is why I walk with my arms folded across my chest, like I'm doing now. There's no one out here on the road—no one on Long Island ever walks anywhere—but still, I hate the feeling of bouncing all over the place. I don't understand those women's lib chicks who braid the hair under their armpits and walk around braless, I really don't. I've been wearing an over-the-shoulder boulder-holder since I was nine and a half.

See, when I was younger, I used to go to sleep-away camp every August. The summer I was nine, I must have had a growth spurt while I was gone, because the first thing Shirley said to me after she hadn't seen me for a month was "Young lady, you go put on a bra right now or else." Like I was committing a crime or something. I didn't even own a bra, for God's sake, so Shirley had to take me shopping. That was a barrel of laughs.

Shirley and I walked into Macy's lingerie department and a saleswoman with a yellow tape measure hanging around her neck like a snake rushed over to us. "Can I help you?" she asked.

"My daughter needs a bra," Shirley said, like this was the worst news she'd ever had to give someone.

But the saleswoman couldn't have been more pleased. "Isn't that wonderful?" she asked, all smiles. "Her first?"

"Yes." Shirley sighed. "You'll have to measure her."

"Lift your arms for me, dear," the saleswoman said,

whipping the tape measure off her neck. Then right there in the middle of the aisle she wrapped the tape measure across my back and pulled it over my breasts and I was so embarrassed I wanted to die.

"Thirty-two. And it looks like she's a B already," the woman announced to me, Shirley, and everyone else in the Tri-State area.

"Thirty-two *B*?" Shirley repeated in this horrified voice, because, for your information, Shirley also wears a size B, a 36B in fact. I happen to know this because I see her bras when I fold the laundry, which is one of my weekly chores. Chores, for crying out loud. You'd think we lived out on the prairie or right here on Bessie's farm.

I put down my knapsack and call Bessie over. And though I try not to, I can't help noticing her udders swinging from side to side. I hate when anyone notices my breasts, and believe me, after that summer, Shirley wasn't the only one who paid attention to them. Mike made a few cracks about "keeping abreast of the situation" until he saw how upset it made me, and then he stopped. Fred never said anything, of course, but he definitely noticed. And he wasn't the only one. Take it from me, every single member of the male species treated me differently from the moment my bazooms entered the picture. Especially Donald Caruso, who for a while acted like his sole purpose on earth was to see how many times a day he could snap my bra strap. And then there was that school trip to Old Sturbridge Village.

Old Sturbridge Village, in case you don't know, is this place in Massachusetts where everything is still like it was two hundred years ago, with the people who work there all dressed up like Pilgrims and stuff. It took forever to get there, and then on the way home it was all dark and I was sitting on the bus by myself because Ronnie was out sick, when Donald Caruso slipped into the seat next to me. Now, this was way before he started going out with Donna Rizzo, and every girl in my whole school had a big crush on him except for yours truly, who couldn't care less. So I just shut my eyes and pretended to be asleep, and the next thing I knew, Donald Caruso had his arm around my shoulders, which was okay, I guess, and then the next thing I knew after that, his hand was on my breast.

You'd think I would have popped him one right on the kisser, and I probably should have. But I didn't. I don't know why. I mean, it never occurred to me that Donald Caruso might actually like me. I couldn't even believe it—me, the least popular girl on Long Island, was going to second base with the most sought-after boy in our entire school.

I guess I was too stunned to do anything but sit there and see what it felt like. It was okay, I guess. Donald was gentle, which surprised me. He just let his hand rest against me so softly, I got a little dreamy and could hardly even tell if I was asleep or not. His hand was soothing, sort of, and I think I almost did fall asleep. Until I heard someone laughing and I opened my eyes to see John Batista, Donald's best friend, leaning over the back of the seat in front of us, looking down with this stupid smirk on his face that made me want to just rip his head off. But instead I just made this little chewing noise, like I really was sleeping and just happened to be switching dreams or something, and then I rolled over toward the window and folded my arms over my chest, and then Donald got up to change his seat and that was the end of that.

Except the next day at school, I felt really weird. God, what a stupid eighth grader I was. I didn't even know if Donald Caruso liked me or not. I mean, we made out on the bus, sort of, and doesn't that mean a guy is your boyfriend? At least, that's what I thought, but when I passed Donald in the hall, a million girls were all over him as usual, and he didn't even say hi to me, and I knew better than to say it first.

God, I don't know why I'm thinking about all this stuff today. I ask Bessie if she thinks I'm losing my mind, but she doesn't answer. I don't know what Bessie thinks, but I definitely know what Shirley thinks. Shirley says I spend too much time by myself, which is a nice way of saying *My daughter's a social reject. Where did I go wrong?* I am kind of a loner, I guess, which between you, me, and this fence post worries me a little. I mean, every murderer I read about in *Newsday* is described as a loner. "He kept to himself" is what all the neighbors who wish to remain anonymous always say.

Not that I have any homicidal tendencies or anything, in case you're getting worried. It's just that I think most human beings aren't really worth my time. The girls in my class? Airheads on heels. The boys? Numbskulls in high-tops. So where does that leave me? Talking to a poor old cow and waving hello to my only friend in the world, a guy in a brown Volkswagen who doesn't even know my name.

THREE

Some days, like today, for example, I wonder why I don't just give in and take the bus. I guess Shirley's right for once in her life—I am stubborn as a mule, like she's always telling me, because it's totally freezing out here and it's only the first week of October. I'm wearing an old jacket of Mike's and I can still feel the wind blowing up my sleeves. But I don't care. Bessie would miss me if I didn't show. And I would miss *him*.

And here he comes. I almost don't hear the Beetle's engine because my sneakers are crunching through all these dead leaves and they make more noise than you'd think, and then there's the wind besides. I wave, as usual, and he waves, as usual . . . and then he stops the car by the side of the road a little ways up ahead.

Oh my God, I can't believe it. I know this is it, the big *it,* the it I've been waiting for my entire life. I knew he'd stop for me, I just knew it. I feel like leaping in the air and kicking my heels together or turning a cartwheel like Donna Rizzo and all the other stupid cheerleaders—like I ever could.

I don't walk any faster or any slower and it seems like it takes forever, you know, like one of those stupid sanitary napkin TV commercials where a woman is running in slow motion on the beach, but finally I get to the car. He's pulled over to the right side of the road, so I have to walk past the driver's side. He's got the window rolled down even though it's freezing, and his elbow is sticking out of the car like a big broken wing. I get up to the car and before I even say hi, a big grin bursts across his face like he just cleaned up on *The Price Is Right* or something. He looks me up and down and says, "Get in, gorgeous," so I do, even though he can't possibly be talking to me. I mean, gorgeous? Who is he kidding? But there's no one else around except Bessie, and I'm sure he's not issuing an invitation to a cow.

I get in the car even though I can practically hear Shirley screaming, *What are you, crazy? How many times have I told you not to talk to strangers, let alone get in a car with one?* But I don't care. And besides, I'm not some two-year-old who can be lured into a kidnapper's car by a lollipop. I'm practically a grown-up; I can take care of myself.

As soon as I plop down into the seat and close the car door, my chauffeur starts to drive. He doesn't bother asking me where I live and I don't bother telling him.

I look out the window and see Bessie watching from the middle of the field. She looks back over her shoulder, her big brown eyes wide with surprise, and then she swats at her face with the tip of her tail. I feel bad for her because I think she looks forward to our talks every day as much as I do, but what can I do? I can't exactly say, *Hey, pal, could you just wait a minute while I say good-bye to my cow?* How stupid would that look? She isn't even my cow.

The Volkswagen's really small, unlike Shirley's Oldsmobile or Fred's Caddie. I mean, there's barely any room in here. And you should see the glove compartment. It looks so small, I bet all you could fit in there is a pair of gloves. My new buddy and I are sitting so close together, we're practically touching. Except the seats are bucket seats and the stick shift is sticking up between us.

I've never been alone in a car with a guy before, and I'm not sure what to do. First of all there's the problem of my knapsack. Right now it's on my lap and it's kind of heavy with all my books in it, but I don't know if I should put it in the backseat or just keep it where it is. I could put it on top of my feet, I guess. The next problem is the seat belt. I probably should buckle up, but I don't want him to think I'm a big baby. If I were driving with the Rents, there would be no question about it: Shirley won't even back out of the driveway unless everyone in the car is all strapped in. Well, I guess I can take a chance and not wear my seat belt for once in my life. What the heck, he's not wearing his.

I settle back in my seat and turn my head a little so I can look over at Mr. Wonderful while he drives. He's kind of good-looking, though not like your typical movie star. He has the most incredible brown eyes I've ever seen, dark as Bessie's, with long lashes, and his hair is dark too, parted on the side and falling over his forehead in front and long in the back, though not as long as Mike's. He doesn't have the greatest skin in the world, but hey, that isn't his fault. It looks like maybe he had acne or chicken pox or something when he was my age and it left his cheeks kind of bumpy. But that only makes him handsome in a rugged, tough guy kind of way. I guess you could say his face has character, you know, like he's been through something but came out on top. He's wearing a navy blue shirt with pants to match, like some kind of uniform that should have his name embroidered over his right breast pocket only it doesn't. I can't really see his shoes.

We drive for a while without talking until he looks over at me and says, "What are you staring at?" as if he didn't know.

"Nothing," I mumble, then turn and look out the window. As I watch cars go by, I feel him looking at me, but I don't say anything until we stop at a red light. Then I say without turning around, "What are you staring at?" just like he did.

"You," he says in such a gentle voice I turn back

around. And there's that happy grin on his face again, like *Bingo!* he just hit the jackpot, which I guess is me.

"How old are you, anyway?" he asks.

"Old enough," I say, and I can tell he thinks so too. We both grin and look at each other hard, as if we're having a staring contest like Ronnie and I used to. I feel a giggle trying to worm its way up my throat so I press my lips together as tight as I can, but the harder I try not to laugh the more I want to. And then just when my face is about to break, the car behind us honks to let us know the light is green. But instead of moving, my guy just keeps staring at me. Then he gives me a wink, lifts his left hand, and flips the bird to the driver behind us. For a second I'm scared it's Shirley on her way to Waldbaum's to pick up some Wonder bread, but then the driver behind us honks again and we pull away too fast for me to turn around, not that I really care.

"Where are we going?" I ask after a few minutes.

"You'll see," he says, which is probably just his polite way of saying "Shut up," so I do, but just for a minute.

"What's your name?" I ask.

"Frank."

"I'm Vanessa," I say, like he cares. I don't even know why I say it. I don't know anyone named Vanessa, but I don't want to say my name because I hate it. Andrea. Gross. Especially the phony way Shirley says it, *On-DRAY-uh,* like I'm the queen of England. I call myself Andi and spell it with an *i,* but I'm afraid Frank will think that's a boy's name, which is what my grandmother thinks.

My grandmother refuses to call me Andi. She calls me Andrea Robin. Robin is my middle name, like Christopher Robin, the kid in *Winnie-the-Pooh,* which was my favorite book when I was little. See, even when I was a baby, I liked animals better than people. I have a ton of stuffed animals in my room, and a million books about animals too, like *Curious George* and *The Story of Babar* from when I was little, and *Black Beauty* and *The Incredible Journey,* which I like so much I read them over at least once a year. But anyway, the point is my grandmother used to read *Winnie-the-Pooh* to me all the time when I was little and whenever it said "Christopher Robin" in the book, she'd say "Andrea Robin" instead. I know it's kind of babyish, but once in a while, I still read *Winnie-the-Pooh*, and whenever it says "Christopher Robin" I say "Andrea Robin" too.

While I'm thinking all this, Frank keeps driving, and just between you, me, and the stick shift, I have no idea where in the world we are. We haven't been driving very long, but still, I wonder what time it is. I never wear a watch, so every time I go somewhere with the Units, I'm always asking Fred what time it is and he always answers, "Why, got a date?" And now I guess I do.

Finally we pull onto this dirt road and Frank stops the car. Then he takes a screwdriver off the dashboard, sticks it into the ignition, and turns it toward him to shut the engine off. I can't believe I didn't even notice we've been driving this whole time without a key in the ignition. Like Frank has magic powers or something. I glance out the window and see we're in front of a white house that looks like your typical, basic two-story Long Island home, only kind of run-down.

"You live here?" I ask.

"Yeah," Frank snorts. "Me and the president. C'mon."

He gets out and I open my door and hesitate. For the first time, I feel a little scared. I mean, just because I wave to Frank every day on the way home from school and he waves back doesn't mean I really know the guy. I don't think he's a total psycho or anything—I doubt he wants to kill me—but what if he's kidnapping me, and I'm going to have to live in this house out in the middle of nowhere for the rest of my life chained to a radiator with nothing to eat but bread and water? Well, that's one way to lose weight, I guess.

I look out at Frank, who's walking up toward the house, and just at that moment he looks back and smiles that award-winning smile of his that warms me like the sun. Then he turns and continues strolling like he's got all day, and for some reason that makes me want to hurry. I scramble out of the car but then stop. What about my knapsack? Should I take it? Yeah, right, like he's going to help me with my homework. I slip my hand inside my pocket and feel my Swiss army knife. I wonder if I could ever protect myself with it. I doubt it; I can't imagine stabbing a perfect stranger, let alone Frank with it, and besides, I hate the sight of blood. Still, I guess it's good I have it on me.

I slam the car door shut and hurry after Frank like a little kid in a department store trying to keep up with his mother before she steps onto an escalator and disappears. But Frank doesn't disappear. He waits for me outside the house, and then when I catch up to him, he opens the front door, bows, and makes this grand, sweeping gesture with his arm. "Ladies first," he says.

"Thank you," I answer, bending my knees into a little curtsey. As soon as I do it, I feel really stupid, but Frank just smiles, ushers me inside, and closes the door behind me.

"Whose house is this, anyway?" I ask once we're inside. We're standing in a hallway surrounded by completely empty rooms. I guess the people who used to live here moved out and the new people haven't moved in yet. I go into the kitchen, which at least has some counters and cabinets and a sink in it, and turn the faucet just for kicks, but nothing comes out. Then I walk through another room with light blue walls and follow Frank up to the second floor. The stairs creak with every step. Three more rooms, all empty, all painted white, and a bathroom with a toilet, which I can tell just from looking at it doesn't even flush.

"Nobody's," Frank says from one of the rooms. His voice sounds spooky, like it's coming from inside the walls of the house itself.

"What?" I ask, walking toward his voice. He's sitting on the floor in one of the empty rooms with his back leaning against a white wall, fishing a red and white pack of Marlboros out of his shirt pocket.

"You asked me whose house this was," Frank reminds me. He taps his pack until a few cigarettes stick out of the top. "Nobody's," he repeats as he takes the cigarette that sticks out the farthest from his pack and bounces it against the palm of his hand. For some reason that makes a shiver start at the small of my back and tremble up my spine. I put my right hand into my pocket and feel around for the lucky pink shell Mike gave me. It's there; I'm safe.

"Smoke?" Frank asks. I sit down beside him, close enough to show I'm not afraid, but not too close since I am a little, and shake my head. I hate cigarettes. Shirley is a one-woman chimney and Fred smokes too, even though he's a dentist and should know better, and our whole house totally reeks.

Frank sticks his cancer stick in his mouth, lights a match, and cups his hand around the flame as he brings it up to the cigarette. He sucks his cheeks in like he's drinking through a straw and then he shakes the match out and tosses it on the floor. For a second I'm scared the whole house will go up in flames but it doesn't. Frank tilts his head back, exhales, and blows out a smoke ring. I'm glad he doesn't just let the smoke stream out of his nostrils the way Shirley does. I think that's the grossest thing in the world.

"Model," Frank says, and I jump a little. What does he mean, model? What does he want me to do, get up and walk across the room like Twiggy even though I'm ten times her size? Yeah, right. I look at him and he gestures with his cigarette, leaving a trail of blue smoke in the air. "Model house. Supposed to be a new neighborhood but the developer went broke, poor sucker." He shrugs, turns away, and takes another drag. Case closed, I guess. Well, that explains the house, anyway. It doesn't belong to anybody. A model house. Like a model child. But how come he gets to come here? When I ask him, he shrugs. "Connections" is all he says.

Frank finishes his cigarette and puts it out against his work boot. Then he stares out in front of him at nothing for a long time. It looks like his eyes are fixed on a spot about two inches in front of his shoes, but there's nothing there. That I can see, anyway. But maybe Frank can see things I can't, like a cat in the dark. Maybe that's another one of his magic powers. I try to fix my gaze on the exact spot he's looking at, but it's hard to tell if I'm successful. I almost think Frank's forgotten I'm even there, but the second I think that, he turns toward me.

"Nice hair," he says, picking up a strand. "I like my women with long hair."

I shiver again, but I'm not cold. *I like my women*. . . . Am I one of Frank's women now? I hope so. How many does he have? No one's ever called me a woman before, let alone *his* woman. Frank examines my hair closely, like it's the most interesting thing on the planet. Which it isn't; it's just hair, dark brown frizzy hair that's almost down to my waist and would be in much better shape if I didn't split my ends when I get nervous.

Frank weaves a hank of my hair in and out of his fingers, which are quite tan. And kind of hairy. His fingernails are dirty and I can tell from how short and ragged they are that he bites them. And there's something wrong with his right pinkie. The top of it is all scarred and wrinkled like it got caught in a meat grinder and his nail is all black and gross-looking. I try not to stare at it, but I'm afraid I'm going to be sick. I'm really squeamish about stuff like that. Like this one time Shirley gave me a tomato to cut up for a salad and I sliced the tip of my finger by accident instead. The minute I saw that first drop of blood I got nauseous and dizzy and if I hadn't grabbed the counter, I definitely would have hit the floor. Not that Shirley cared. She was more concerned with how much blood I was getting on her brand-new yellow dish towel than with the fact that I almost fainted and was practically bleeding to death.

Anyway, Frank must be able to tell I'm feeling a little funny because he grins at me, lifts a handful of my hair, and tickles my face with it. I try not to laugh but I can't help smiling in spite of myself.

"Old enough," Frank mumbles, and then in half a second he's on top of me. I'm so surprised I freeze for a second before I try to push him off. But it's impossible, so I try to at least get away from the wall, because my neck is all bent out of shape at this crazy angle and the last thing I need right now is my head falling off. I can tell Frank likes the struggle—I can just hear him saying, *I like my women feisty*—so I keep it up even after I'm lying flat on the floor. Frank's still on top of me, and I like the way his body feels. It reminds me of the lead shield my father puts over me at his office (he calls it the Fred Shield) when he X-rays my teeth. It's nice and heavy. Comforting, like a big blanket on a rainy day.

"Ever kiss a smoker?" Frank asks.

Only Fred and Shirley, I think, but I'm sure that's not what he means. Frank takes my chin in his hand and moves my head so I have to look directly into his eyes, but he doesn't hurt me or anything. I've never kissed a guy before, period, but I'm certainly not going to tell him that.

"Like kissing an ashtray," he says.

Gross, I think. *Thanks for the warning.* I wait, but Frank doesn't kiss me; he just lowers his face so close to mine I almost stop breathing. We stare at each other hard again, the way we did in the car, and now I can see he's looking for something, but what? Fear? I'm not afraid. Desire? He's the one who wants something. Frank is so close I can see a tiny version of my whole face reflected in his beautiful brown eyes: a little me in his right eye and a little me in his left eye. The last thing I want to see right now is myself, so I shut my eyes to wait. I don't wait long.

"This your boyfriend's jacket?" Frank asks as he starts to unsnap it. Each snap opens with a little pop.

"My brother's," I say. "I don't have a boyfriend." I spit out the word *boyfriend* like a gulp of milk gone sour in my mouth.

Frank doesn't respond to this, just lays open the sides of Mike's jacket carefully, like he's unwrapping a birthday present. Then he unbuttons my sweater slowly, like we have all the time in the world, and that makes me want to scream. I'm wearing a black cardigan over a black T-shirt and when all my buttons are finally unbuttoned, Frank folds back both sides of my sweater gently, as if they're two pieces of tissue paper covering something delicate. I keep my eyes closed while he's doing all this, but I can see him by looking out from underneath my eyelids.

Frank is kneeling now and staring at me. I feel pretty ridiculous just lying here half undressed but I can tell that even though I'm right in front of him, he's not really seeing me. His eyes are blank, like he's thinking about something or remembering something or trying to make up his mind about something, but I have no idea what. I wonder if I should do something—I mean, what would a girl really named Vanessa do?—but I don't move. I just wait. The back of me is warm against the floor but the front of me is cold, and it's a strange feeling. Like sitting with your back to a warm campfire on a chilly night at the end of August on the last day of sleepaway camp.

Finally Frank shakes his head a little, like he's coming back to life, and then he lifts up my T-shirt. I have to arch my back so it doesn't get stuck and then it's all bunched up under my chin and armpits so my breasts are exposed. Ta-dah. There they are. Under my JCPenney bra, of course.

Frank doesn't touch me and I wonder how long he's going to just stare at me. I suck in my stomach while he studies me. I think he kind of likes me. I hope so, anyway. He seems totally mesmerized by my hooters, which is a good sign. I wonder if he wants me to take off my bra. I mean, am I supposed to be doing something here or what? Just as I'm about to ask, Frank leans down and does the strangest thing. He runs the tip of his finger from my right armpit to my left hip bone and then from my left armpit to my right hip bone, making a big X across my front. Like X marks the spot. And that's it.

I keep lying there waiting for him to do something else, but he doesn't. And then after a minute, Frank gets up. He doesn't say anything, so I just stay where I am with my eyes half closed, still waiting. Then I hear the strike of a match and smell a cigarette, so I guess he's done with me.

I sit up and pull my T-shirt down, button my sweater, and snap my jacket, doing everything Frank did, only in reverse. I still don't know what to do and I'm kind of disappointed. Is that it? Maybe Frank wanted to do more but once he got a good look at me, he didn't like what he saw. Maybe he likes his women skinny instead of flabby like me.

"C'mere." Frank's staring out the window and I get up and go stand next to him. He puts one arm around my shoulders and gathers me close. "You're a good kid," he says, which makes me feel about two years old. I don't want to be a kid. I want to be one of his women.

"I'm not a kid," I mumble into his shirt. "How old are you, anyway?" My guess is around thirty.

"Old enough," he says, and then he grinds out his cigarette on the windowsill, which is really gross. God, smokers get on my nerves sometimes, they really do. I'm always picking up after Shirley, and right now I'm tempted to pocket Frank's butt, but that might make him mad, so I don't.

Frank turns and heads downstairs and I follow him

because I don't know what else to do. He holds the front door open for me, shuts it, and then checks to make sure it's all closed up tight, which is stupid since it's not like there's anything to steal in there. Then we walk back to the car without saying anything and get in. Frank sticks his screwdriver into the ignition and pumps the gas pedal. I wonder where we're going now, not that I really care. Frank doesn't say anything and neither do I, though I'm dying to know: does he like me or what?

Just when I'm about to ask where we are, things start looking familiar. There's the sign for the Long Island Expressway that some stupid kid spray-painted so it says Eggs Zit instead of Exit, like that's really clever. And then we pass the turn to my school and then we're back on Farm Hill Road and Frank stops the car in the exact same spot where he picked me up. I put my hand on the car door, but I don't open it right away. Frank just sits there, staring at me. I wish he would say something. Like what—*I had a great time*? Yeah, right. I want to tell him something like *Thanks for the ride,* or *It was nice meeting you,* or even *See ya,* but before I can even get one word out, Frank says, with that smile that makes my stomach turn over, "Tomorrow."

Tomorrow. The most wonderful word in the English language. *Tomorrow.* The way he says it, it's not a question and it's not a command. It's just a simple fact, a statement, you know, like the sky is blue; tomorrow will come; Frank will drive up, and off I'll go with him.

"Tomorrow," I repeat, nodding in agreement, like I think tomorrow's a wonderful idea, which I do. Then I pick up my knapsack and get out of the car, closing the door gently as though I'm afraid it might break. Frank drives away and gives me the same old wave he's been giving me for the past month like today's just another ordinary day, and I wave back in my usual way, too, like nothing at all has changed. Yeah, right.

FOUR

Home, bittersweet home. I unlock the door, and as soon as I push it open, the burglar alarm starts blaring so loudly I bet my grandmother can hear it all the way down in Florida. Without her hearing aid on.

"Andrea, is that you?" Shirley screams from the living room.

"Yeah, yeah, it's me, it's me." I run to shut off the alarm, then dash into the kitchen to call the cops and give them our secret password so they know it's only us screwing up again and they don't have to rush over.

"I'm sorry," I yell after I hang up the phone.

"Andrea, come in here, please."

Uh-oh. I drag myself into the living room, where Shirley is watching *The Edge of Night, One Life to Live,* or some other stupid soap opera.

"I'm sorry," I say again before she can start yelling at me. "I didn't do it on purpose. I just forgot to turn it off before I opened the door."

"That's beside the point," Shirley says, barely taking her eyes off the TV. "Why can't you be more careful? The police have better things to do than respond to every false alarm in the neighborhood. You've got to focus on what you're doing, Andrea. Why are you so distracted?"

You don't want to know, I think. Out loud I say, "Well, at least I remembered the password," unlike Mike, who set the alarm off last year when he arrived home to surprise Shirley for her birthday. Since we weren't expecting him, Mike came home to an empty house and when he set off the alarm he had no idea what was happening. (Mike swears we never told him about the burglar alarm; Fred swears we did. My guess is that Fred's right but Mike was probably so stoned at the time it didn't register.) Anyway, when the cops came and asked Mike the secret password, all he kept saying was "Hey, c'mon. I live here, man." Well, the cops took one look at him with his long hair and ratty clothes and said, "Sure you do, buddy." And then they hauled him right off to the station. I bet Shirley will never forget that birthday.

"I'm sorry," I apologize to Shirley for the third time. "It won't happen again."

"It better not," Shirley says. "Now go get me a pack of cigarettes, will you? My nerves are shot."

Ever the dutiful daughter, I go into the kitchen and open the drawer where most people keep their silverware but where we keep cigarettes—Virginia Slims for Shirley and Lucky Strikes for Fred. "Another twenty nails for your coffin," I say softly so Shirley won't hear, since the one time I said it out loud she took away my allowance for two weeks.

"Here," I say, bringing the pack into the living room.

"Thank you." Shirley takes the cigarettes and looks up to give me the once-over. "Oh, Andrea, do you have to wear pants with patches on the knees to school?" She sighs dramatically. "If you need new clothes, I've told you a hundred times I'd be happy to take you shopping. We could go right now."

"For your information, this is a style, Shirley," I tell her. "All the kids at school wear pants like this."

"Some style." Shirley strikes a match and lights her cigarette. "Your father works extremely hard, Andrea, and I'm sure he doesn't appreciate his daughter running around looking like we're two steps away from the poorhouse. And what happened to that nice pocketbook I bought you? Do you have to go around with that worn-out knapsack on your back like a hobo?"

"Yes."

"Well, it doesn't do anything for you, Andrea, if you know what I mean." Shirley directs her attention back to the TV and I study her as she watches her show and puffs away. She holds her cigarette between the second and third fingers of her left hand. Her fingers are long and slender and her nails are shiny and red, courtesy of her once-a-week appointment at the beauty parlor. And on her fourth finger she wears this band of diamonds that Fred gave her for their twentieth anniversary, instead of the plain gold wedding band he gave her the day they got hitched. She keeps that ring in a velvet box at the bottom of her underwear drawer. The new ring is nice and everything, and you can tell it cost a mint, but I like the old one better. Sometimes I look at it when I put away the laundry. When I was younger, I used to like trying it on, but now it only fits my pinky because compared to Shirley, I'm an elephant, as she constantly reminds me.

"What did you have for lunch today?" Shirley asks during an Alka-Seltzer commercial, as if on cue.

I rack my brain. "Um, an apple and a Dannon vanilla yogurt."

"Good." Shirley nods her approval. If she knew I'd had macaroni and cheese, a brownie, *and* a chocolate chip cookie, she would kill me.

"I went to Mrs. Goodman's for lunch," Shirley tells me, like I care. "She served us fondue, isn't that interesting? Cheese fondue for the main course and chocolate fondue for dessert. Everyone got these cute little forks to dip chunks of bread and fruit with. It was delicious, Andrea. Of course, I have to go right back on Weight Watchers tomorrow, but it was worth it. Maybe I'll make it sometime, but I'm not sure your father would like it. What do you think? You know his taste. Do you think he'd enjoy it?"

"Whatever." I mean, how should I know if Fred would like fondue or not? Besides, it's a moot point, since

Shirley hasn't cooked a real meal since TV dinners were invented.

"Your father is such a meat-and-potatoes man," Shirley goes on. "You can cook meat in it too. Maybe I'll try that. . . . " Her voice trails off.

"I'm going to start my homework," I say, turning to leave.

"Can you change the channel?" Shirley points at the TV with the tip of her cigarette. God forbid she should get off the couch and change it herself. "Put on channel two. I want to see who's on *The Mike Douglas Show*."

After I change the channel, I go upstairs to my room and put a Janis Joplin album that Mike left behind when he went off to college on my record player. Then I flop down on my bed, but before I even have time to take off my sneakers and relax, Shirley yells up the stairs, "Andrea! Turn that screeching down!"

"It's not screeching. It's singing," I yell back before I turn the volume knob a hundredth of an inch to the left. I wait a minute, and when Shirley doesn't yell again, I lie back down on my bed, shut my eyes, listen to Janis, and think about Frank. Oh my God, I can't believe what happened to me today. A guy—no, a *man*—whisked me off and had his way with me. Well, sort of. You have to admit what he did was pretty weird, but he didn't hurt me or anything. He just ran the tip of his finger down my stomach like he was checking to see if it was dusty. But who cares? He was really sweet and gentle, especially when he put his arms around me over by the window and we just stood there being quiet. It felt peaceful, like when I hang out by the fence with Bessie. Most people don't know how to just be still like that. I'm glad Frank does.

I reach over for Snowball, my favorite stuffed animal, and hug the soft white cat to my chest. "Do you think Frank and I will fall in love and live happily ever after?" I whisper into her ear. Then I move her head up and down like she's saying yes. Hey, don't laugh; it could happen. Donna Rizzo is totally convinced she's going to walk down the aisle with good old Donald Caruso. I wonder if Frank is even the marrying type. He strikes me more as the living-together type, which is no big deal. I don't care about a stupid piece of paper, though believe me, it wasn't the greatest idea in the world to tell the Parental Units that.

It was a Sunday morning, and the three of us were sitting around the kitchen table eating bagels spread with this putrid low-fat cream cheese that Shirley insists on buying, and reading sections of the *New York Times*. Shirley was reading the wedding announcements and Fred was reading the obituaries, which tells you something, but I don't know what.

"So guess who's getting married?" Shirley asked out loud.

"The Pope?" I asked back.

"Very funny." Shirley shook her head. "Fred, take a guess."

"I give up," Fred said.

"Karen Blumenthal. And her picture's right here in the *Times*. Isn't that something?"

"Who's Karen Blumenthal?" Fred and I asked at the same time, though neither one of us really cared.

"Alice and Sid's daughter. You know, they live over on Garden Lane? That's going to be quite an affair." Shirley licked her lips as though she could already taste the high-calorie fancy food the Blumenthals were sure to serve. "They certainly can afford it. But don't worry, Andrea," Shirley added. "When the time comes, we'll go all out for you."

"I'm not getting married," I said, reaching for another half a bagel, but Shirley stopped me cold with one of her "you don't need that" looks.

"What do you mean you're not getting married? Of course you're getting married. Everyone gets married." Shirley's voice went up a zillion decibels as she went totally bananas.

"Okay, okay, don't wig out, I'm getting married," I said, just so she'd get off my case. "But I'm going to be barefoot and have wildflowers in my hair and my dog will be the ring bearer and it'll be up on top of a mountain and . . . "

"Andrea." Shirley let out this huge sigh like the entire world had just come to an end. She took a big gulp of her coffee, which was a disgusting shade of gray from the skim milk she puts in it instead of cream, and then addressed my father. "You're going to have a lot of trouble with your daughter," she said. As opposed to saying *our* daughter. Like Fred gave birth to me all by himself.

I put Snowball down, turn over Mike's Janis Joplin album, which is skipping—no wonder he didn't take it up to Buffalo—and start my homework. But even though I have two French lessons to go over and a ton of math problems to solve, I can't force myself to pick up a pencil. All I can do is think about Frank.

Let's say, just for kicks, that we do get married, or at least wind up living together. What will I tell our children about the day we met? "Well, kids, your father pulled off to the side of the road and I got in his car and he took me to this empty house and drew a big fat X on my big fat stomach." So much for telling them not to talk to strangers, like Shirley and Fred are always telling me. Which makes no sense because everyone's a stranger until you talk to them, right? So if you never talked to strangers, how would you make any friends? I'll give you an example: last year Shirley and Fred went on a cruise to the Virgin Islands, which is a weird name for a place— what do they have there, a bunch of girls who haven't done it yet, like me? Anyway, there they were on a boat in the middle of the ocean with a bunch of strangers and they all started talking to each other and by the time they got off the boat they were all the best of friends. When I said to Fred, "But that's talking to strangers," he said that was different, but I didn't see what was so different about it. Just because they all have money and are on the same cruise ship doesn't mean they can't be lunatics or criminals or killers.

It's useless to even pretend I'm doing my homework, so I get up from my desk and flop down on my bed again. The question that's going around my mind is: why did Frank pick me? I'm not exactly a prize or anything. Like I already told you, I'm kind of chunky, and I'm not exactly the smartest kid on the planet.

I wonder how old Frank is. Not that it really matters or anything. I'm just curious. If he's around thirty, he's fifteen years older than I am, which isn't as big a deal as you might think. I mean, when I'm eighty, he'll be ninety-five, and who cares by then? Frank would probably kill me if he knew I was only fifteen. I know I look older on account of my boobs. I'll be sixteen soon, in December.

I jump off my bed—I just can't sit still today—and look at myself in the full-length mirror behind my door. Slowly, I unbutton my sweater and lift up my T-shirt, trying to see what Frank saw. There's my stomach, white and flabby as ever. I don't know what I expected, maybe that it would be marked or something, but it's not. I suck it in and wish it would just stay like that, but I have to breathe eventually and then it pops back out. Maybe I should lose a little weight so Frank will like me better.

I go over to my desk, take a piece of paper out of a drawer, and write *Frank and Andrea* on it inside a little heart with an arrow going through it and the whole bit. It takes me a minute to remember, and when I do, I crumple it up, take out another piece of paper and write *Frank and Vanessa* instead. Vanessa. God, where in the world did I ever come up with that one? "Sometimes you just kill me, Andrea Robin," I say out loud to myself. "You really, really do."

✖ ✖ ✖

The problem is Bessie. Now that I actually have somewhere to go after school, I won't have a chance to hang out with her. So I decide to see her before school. It means

I have to leave a little earlier in the morning, but I don't care and the Units won't even notice. Fred usually leaves for the office at the crack of dawn before I'm even up, and Shirley doesn't rise and shine until after I leave for school because, as she puts it, she needs her beauty sleep.

I set my alarm twenty minutes earlier and I'm up and out at the ungodly hour of quarter after seven. Though why they call it ungodly is beyond me. If I believed in God, I'd think it was kind of godly right now, with everything nice and quiet for a change and the sky all blue-gray like it only is before the day begins.

Bessie's in her field, and when I call her, she comes right over like she isn't surprised to see me at all. I pull up some grass and let her take it out of my hand.

"Listen, Bessie," I say as she chomps away. "I can't see you so much anymore because now I have a boyfriend." She gives me this look like she doesn't believe me or maybe she does but she doesn't really care, and then she goes right on chewing. For some reason, this makes me incredibly sad. You'd think I'd be happy, for God's sake; I mean, something exciting is finally happening to me, somebody finally *likes* me, which is a total miracle, but I actually get all teary, like we're really saying good-bye.

"Listen, Bessie," I say again, ripping up more grass for her, "we'll always be friends, right? You know that. It's just, well, you know." She takes the grass from my hand, and I swear to God, she nods like she does understand, and that makes me a million times sadder than I already am. So I just stand there, petting her back and letting the tears roll down my cheeks.

"Frank and I . . . " I drop my voice to a whisper even though no one's around to hear. "Frank and I just need to be together, you know? I mean, I'm almost sixteen, I have to have some kind of life besides talking to a cow." All of a sudden I have this mad urge to just haul off and belt her one, I really do. Why should I care about some stupid old cow? So I give her a good shove just to see if I can make her fall over, but nothing happens. It's like shoving a brick wall. I expected her to go down in a heap of old bones but she doesn't move an inch. *Stubborn as a mule,* I think, which is how Shirley describes me. Maybe she should really say stubborn as a cow.

I give Bessie another push, but my heart's not in it and she just looks at me with those big brown eyes of hers like I'm a real imbecile, which I guess I am.

"Look," I tell her, "I have to go." I pull up one last handful of grass and hold it out to Bessie like a peace offering. She takes it and chews it up while I walk away without looking back.

✖ ✖ ✖

Frank's waiting for me after school like he promised. I see his brown Volkswagen as soon as I turn the corner, and for some reason half of me wants to run to the car as fast as I can and the other half of me wants to turn around and run the other way. I don't know what's wrong with me. I mean, a guy finally likes me, so what is my problem?

I walk right over to the car, open the door, and fling my knapsack into the backseat like it belongs there. Then I get in and Frank pulls away before I close the door without saying a word. No *Hello*. No *How was your day, dear?* I don't say anything either. I just listen to this crazy song going round and round in my head: *Over the river and through the woods, to nobody's house we go.* That is, I assume we're going to the same place we went yesterday, since I haven't been told otherwise.

I wonder if I should say something to Frank, but what? It's funny—I always wanted to find someone I could just be quiet with, somebody who didn't fill up every single second with stupid small talk like Shirley. And now that I have found someone, all this quiet makes me nervous.

While Frank drives, I pick up a strand of my hair and start searching for split ends, which is what I always do when I'm feeling antsy. I know it's a bad habit, but at least it's not going to kill me, like smoking. I split a few ends and then decide I'll wait until we go through three traffic lights, and if he doesn't say anything by then, I'll say . . . what? I don't know. God, I feel like a dumb blonde except my hair is brown, which is just another example of how I can't do anything right.

We go through one green light and then another one and then when we get to the third light it turns red, and Frank shifts gears, comes to a stop, and puts his hand on my leg, which feels comforting, like when you put your hand on a dog's head to reassure it. Only I wish it wasn't Frank's right hand, which is the one that has the weird pinkie. I try not to stare at it, but then I force myself to because I have to get used to his finger being all messed up if I'm going to be with him. I wonder how it happened, but I know better than to ask.

Frank's hand is making my leg feel all tingly. I wish

my thighs weren't so fat—they look like a hippo's compared to Frank's—but he doesn't seem to notice, or if he does, I guess he doesn't care. He just keeps his hand where it is and I wonder if I'm supposed to do something, like hold it. The light turns green and Frank takes his hand away. He moves the stick shift, pulls out, and puts his hand back on my leg, a little higher this time. I look over at him with a question in my eyes, but he just smiles.

We pull up to the house and Frank cuts the engine with his screwdriver. I get out of the car before he does and then I don't know what to do. I should have waited for Frank to make the first move. He's still sitting in the driver's seat staring out the window like there's something there to see. Which there isn't. It looks like he's thinking about something but I have no idea what. Maybe he doesn't really like me. Maybe he's sorry he picked me up but he doesn't know how to tell me.

God, if Frank breaks up with me, I'll just kill myself, I really will. You probably think I'm nuts since I just met the guy yesterday, but I just know my whole life is going to be different from now on. That's what they say, right, that love changes everything. Puts a smile on your face, gives you a reason to get up in the morning. Like today, I didn't even mind being in school so much, knowing that after the last bell rang, I was going to see Frank. I didn't even lose it when Donald Caruso plowed into me on the lunch line and spilled orange soda all over my tray. Why should I care what that jerk does when I have more important things going on in my life? At least I think I do. *Oh, please, Frank, just get out of the car,* I silently say to him. *Please. Please.* Please.

Oh my God, it works. Frank is actually getting out of the car. He shuts the door and pauses for a moment to give me that smile of his that lets me know we're the only two people in the world that matter. Then he turns and heads for the house with his hands shoved deep in his pockets. I follow like a happy puppy, but not too closely, listening to our feet crunch up the driveway.

Frank goes inside, and I do too. He closes the door behind us, walks into the kitchen, and hoists himself onto the counter without looking at me. I hope he doesn't want me to sit there next to him; I doubt I could get myself up there. It's kind of high and I don't want to make a fool of myself trying. So I just stand there and wait. Frank takes his time lighting his Marlboro, shaking it from the pack, hitting it against his hand, you know, the usual routine. He doesn't offer me one like he did yesterday, which is too bad, because I was thinking maybe I'd try it. Even though I think smoking is disgusting, there's got to be something to it, right? I mean, Shirley thinks cigarettes are the greatest invention since dishwashers, and Frank definitely enjoys puffing away, so I must be missing out on something. It's funny, most people have a cigarette after sex. At least, in the movies. Not before sex. Or whatever it is we're going to do.

After about seventeen hours, Frank finally finishes his cigarette. I'm totally relaxed by now, like I'm the one who had a smoke—at least, that's what Shirley says: there's nothing like a cigarette to calm your nerves—but then Frank stubs his butt out on the counter and I start to feel nervous again.

"Didn't anyone ever tell you never to get in a car with a stranger?" Frank asks, staring at the floor.

What a weird question for him to ask me. I mean, what does he think, he's my father now? I don't bother answering him because this has got to be his idea of a joke. What am I supposed to say? *Yeah, Frank, about a hundred million times.*

"Are you scared of me?" he asks. This time he looks at me and I can tell he wants me to say something.

"Should I be?" The question pops out of my mouth before I can stop it.

"C'mere," he says, so I go over to him. I guess because I didn't answer his question, he's not going to answer mine. I stand right in front of him, and we stare at each other. He's wearing the same thing as yesterday, blue shirt and pants, but he's got a black jacket on too. "So," he says, "you don't have a boyfriend."

Even though it isn't a question, I answer, "No." But then I think, *Wait a minute—yes, I do. His name is Frank.*

"Have you ever kissed a boy?"

God, I don't want to say no. He'll think I'm a total loser. But if I say yes, what if he asks me who? "No"—I opt for the truth—"but a boy felt me up once."

"Did you like it?" Frank asks. He looks me in the eye.

"No," I say to the floor. Frank doesn't say anything else, and even though I don't want to, I start thinking about that time on the bus with Donald Caruso and stupid John Batista looking over the back of the seat, and then to my absolute and total horror, a sob rises in my throat and I start to cry.

"Poor little girl." Frank pulls me toward him and holds me close. I'm standing between his legs, and the edge of the counter is digging into my big fat stomach, but I don't care.

"Did he hurt you, baby?" Frank asks softly, and I just shake my head because I'm practically sobbing now. I'm so embarrassed, I want to die; I'm getting snot all over the front of his jacket and everything, but Frank is really nice about it. He strokes the back of my hair like he's petting a dog and holds me against him, leaning his cheek against the side of my head. Then he hugs me with both arms real tight and says right into my ear, "Listen, doll, I don't want you going out with any boys your own age, you hear me? They don't know the first thing about how to treat a beautiful woman like you."

I can't believe my ears. Did Frank just call me beautiful?

"Take off your jacket." Frank opens his arms so I can step back. I wish he would take my clothes off, like yesterday, but I guess for some reason he's not going to, so I yank the left side of Mike's jacket open. The snaps pop real fast, like fireworks.

"Take off your sweater."

I whip my V-neck over my head.

"Keep going."

Keep going? Does Frank want me to take off my pants or my bra? I know better than to ask. My guess is he wants to see my breasts. I take off my bra and consider twirling it around in a circle over my head like a stripper, but of course I don't.

"Wow." Frank stares, bug-eyed, and lets out a little whistle, of appreciation, I guess, and I have to say, I am kind of proud. I don't know why; it's not like I did anything, they just grew all by themselves. But they *are* mine.

Frank hops off the counter and lands on the floor with a little thud. I start to cross my arms over my chest, but then I make myself put them back down at my sides. Frank comes over, turns me around, and lifts me up by the waist onto the counter. For some reason I'm a little nervous and I almost laugh.

But Frank is very serious. "The difference between a boy and a man is that a man knows it's more important for his woman to be happy than it is for him to be happy." A minute or so passes while I absorb this, and then Frank says the most amazing thing: "Has anyone ever told you how beautiful you are?"

I shake my head and wait for him to start telling me how beautiful I am, but he doesn't. Instead, he feels me up, and it's not like that time with Donald Caruso in the bus at all. No, it's amazing. It's like I'm an M&M melting in Frank's hands or a lump of sugar dissolving in a cup of tea. My legs get all shaky like Jell-O, they really do. I guess all the corny things they say about being in love are absolutely true.

"You're amazing, Vanessa," Frank says, looking up at me with a grin. Then he turns away and I just sit there, since I don't know what else to do. Frank lights a cigarette and then turns back around and gives me this weird look, like he's almost surprised to see me sitting there.

"Get dressed," he says in this hard voice like he's fed up with me. When I don't move, he barks, "Move it, move it," like he's a drill sergeant.

"Okay, okay," I say, jumping off the counter. "Frank, what'd I do?" I ask, trying not to sound as freaked out as I feel. God, what did I do wrong now?

"Nothing." Frank softens his voice a little. "Just get dressed." He picks up my clothes from the floor and tosses them to me. I do what I'm told and then race out of the house because Frank has already gone down the stairs and out the door without waiting for me.

"Hey, Frank," I yell, but he ignores me and just keeps walking toward the car, so I start to run after him. He wouldn't just leave me here, would he? Then what would I do?

"Frank, what's the matter?" I ask as I slip into the Volkswagen next to him, but he doesn't say a thing. Oh my God, is it over? Frank is so moody. One minute he's the nicest guy on the planet and the next minute he's a big fat jerk. He shoves the screwdriver into the ignition and the car makes this horrible wheezing sound like it's just about to die.

"That stupid scumbag Lloyd," Frank snarls as he jiggles the screwdriver around.

"Who's Lloyd?" I ask, even though I know I shouldn't.

"My partner in crime," Frank mumbles, which I guess is his way of saying friend. "That jerk was supposed to fix this after he . . ." Frank's voice trails off.

"After he what?"

"Never mind," Frank says in his "don't ask any more questions" tone of voice.

Finally, just when I think I'm going to have to walk home, the engine catches. Frank floors it and throws the screwdriver onto the dash. He doesn't say one word to me the whole way back, and believe me, I know better than to start a conversation.

When Frank stops the car at the farm, I reach for my knapsack, kind of stalling, but he still doesn't say anything, so I clear my throat and ask, "Will I see you tomorrow?"

"That's for me to know and you to find out," he says like a total five-year-old. I just look at him but he doesn't say anything else, so then there's nothing to do but get out of the car, slam the door, and wait until tomorrow. Frank sure is a puzzle. First he's nice as can be and then he's totally mean all in the space of an hour and a half. God, leave it to me to fall in love with Dr. Jekyll and Mr. Hyde.

FIVE

"Hello, Kaplan, what are you, deaf?"

"Huh?" I look up from my science quiz to see Stephen Taubman, whose enormous overgrown Jew-fro blocks my view of the blackboard, all turned around in his seat staring at me.

"May I have that, please?" Mrs. Markson is standing right next to my desk with her hand stretched out, and by her tone of voice, I can tell this is at least the third time she's asked me to hand over my paper.

I turn in my unfinished quiz, ask to be excused, and skedaddle into the girls' room for a little peace and quiet. I just want to think for a few minutes, so I lock myself into a stall and play yesterday's events over and over in my mind, like an old, scratched record that keeps skipping. But I just can't figure out what I did wrong. I let Frank go to second base with me, didn't I? Maybe I should have gone further. I don't want him to think I'm a cocktease, which is something guys supposedly hate. But on the other hand, according to Donna Rizzo, the only way to hold on to a guy is to refuse to go all the way with him. Because once you do, he'll think you're a slut and drop you like a hot curling iron.

The bell rings and before I can make my great escape, the door bangs open and a horde of girls comes pouring in. I don't feel like dealing with anybody so I stay where I am, wishing they would all go away. But of course they don't.

"God, I wish I'd get my period," I hear someone say. It's Cheryl Healy; I recognize her whiny, high-pitched voice. And we all know she doesn't mean she wishes she'd get her period the way Hillary Jacoby wishes she'd get hers—she's the only girl in our class who hasn't gotten her friend yet. Cheryl Healy with her see-through blouses and her so-short-half-her-butt-sticks-out miniskirts is the biggest tramp in the whole school and she has a pregnancy scare just about every month. Plus she's really mean, too. Rumor has it that years ago she cut off her own sister's eyelashes just because she felt like it. And her sister didn't do anything; she was just minding her own business in her crib, fast asleep.

"I'm late too," another voice says, bragging a little. That's got to be Diane Carlson, Cheryl's best friend.

"Oh, girls," says a voice full of pity that belongs to none other than Donna Rizzo. "If you just had a little bit of common sense, you wouldn't be having these problems." Clearly Donna feels like she's better than the rest of the world because she won't let her boyfriend lay a hand on her until they're actually married, or at least officially engaged. Which is probably why Donald Caruso is so obnoxious. I mean, if the poor guy could just get some action besides kissing, he'd probably calm down a little. I don't know why he doesn't just give her an ultimatum—screw me or screw you—but hey, what do I know about love?

I hear the strike of a match and then Cheryl says, "Care for a smoke, Donna?" Which is a joke, since Donna Rizzo would probably put Donald Caruso's you-know-what in her mouth before she ever let a cigarette touch her lips.

"Gross! Cheryl Healy and Diane Carlson, you put those cigarettes out right now," Donna says, and then starts coughing like she's about to lose a lung.

"What's the matter, Donna, got a frog in your throat?" Cheryl says, which makes me laugh out loud. Oops. Big mistake.

"Hey, who's in there?" Cheryl Healy asks. Since the jig is up, I flush the toilet I didn't use and slink out of the stall.

"Well, if it isn't Mondo Busto," Cheryl says with a chuckle. She and Diane rest their cigarettes on the windowsill and then, as if on cue, they raise their fists in front of their chests with their elbows pointing out, pull back their arms in a steady pumping rhythm, and start chanting:

> "We must! We must!
> We must increase our bust!
> The bigger the better, the tighter the sweater!
> We must! We must!"

"Ha, ha, very funny," I say, going over to the sink to wash my hands even though I don't really need to.

"Oh, never mind," Cheryl says as she and Diane quit with the calisthenics and pick up their smokes. "Anything over a mouthful is just a waste anyway."

"That's what you think," I say, reaching for a paper towel.

"Is that so, Miss My Cups Runneth Over?" Cheryl blows a puff of smoke at my back. "Tell us all about it."

"This I've got to hear," Diane Carlson says as she and Cheryl close in on me. But before I can open my big fat mouth again, the door bangs open, Donna Rizzo marches out, and two seconds later someone else marches in clearing her throat.

"Are there students smoking in here?" It's Mrs. Markson, standing in the doorway with her hands on her hips. "All right, you three. To the principal's office. March."

"But"—I shut off the water and try to protest—"I wasn't—"

"No, ifs, ands, or cigarette *butts,*" Mrs. Markson says, fanning her hand in front of her face. "Let's go."

"You're dead, Kermit," Cheryl hisses to Donna Rizzo,

who smirks as we pass her in the hall. Luckily the principal lets me off with a warning since I'm a first-time offender, and I'm only a little late to math, my last class of the day. I just sit there in a fog, waiting for class to end, and when it finally does, you'd think I'd rush down the hall, out the door, and over to Farm Hill Road to see if Frank's there or not, but I just go at my usual pace. Either he'll be there or he won't, so who cares if I walk fast or slow?

When I turn onto Farm Hill Road, I know without even looking that Frank's not there. It's not even that I don't hear his motor running, it's just this sinking feeling I have in my stomach, like I just ate a hundred matzo balls that my grandmother made for Passover, which weigh about a pound and a half apiece. I can't believe it's all over. The best thing that ever happened to me in my entire life. *Finito.* Done. The End.

There's nothing for me to do but walk over to Bessie's fence, but I don't even click my tongue to call her over. I'm too depressed to do anything but stand here and pick at my split ends. They're easy to see with the sun shining on my hair, and who cares if I wreck it now that Frank is gone?

I wish I had someone to talk to about all this. But who, Shirley? Yeah, right. For all Shirley knows, I don't have a clue about the birds and the bees. When I told Shirley I got my period she said, "Oh God, already?" like I'd done it too soon. Like I could help it. Then she gave me a box of pads and spent a good twenty minutes showing me how to wash out my underwear (cold water and

Woolite does the trick). And that was our big mother-daughter talk about the facts of life. And Fred is even worse. He'd totally kill me if he knew about Frank. Fred thinks I'm his private property or something. Like once when I was eleven, I asked him when I could start dating. He said, "When you're thirty-five," but he was only kidding. I think.

So who's left—Mike? I don't know if I'd even tell Mike about Frank. Most girls don't get along with their older brothers, but Mike and I have been tight ever since I was a baby. When Shirley used to walk me in my carriage, Mike trotted along right beside her, helping her push it. And when someone came up to check me out, Mike would point to himself and say in this tough-guy voice, "That's *my* sister. You can look but you better not touch." God, I wish Mike were still around. Mike left home the minute he could and he hardly ever comes to visit. We talk on the phone sometimes, but it's just not the same.

If Ronnie hadn't moved away, I'd probably tell her about Frank, but Ronnie's gone. Pennsylvania, for God's sake. I miss her so much. You know how when someone looks really sad and someone else says to her, "What's the matter? You look like you lost your best friend?" Well, I *have* lost my best friend. Ronnie and I were pretty much inseparable. We spent so much time together that Donald Caruso called us lezzies. Or rather, he called me a lezzie, which is really stupid because if *I* was one, then Ronnie would have to be one too, right? And now even with Ronnie gone, Donald still teases me about being a lesbian, always asking me where my girlfriend is in that stupid tone of voice he uses. I wish Donald could meet Frank. Then he'd shut up about me being queer in two seconds flat.

I guess I should just go home, but I don't exactly want to. And besides, my feet feel like they weigh about three hundred pounds. Each. I want to sink down into the ground and never move again, but just when I'm about to give in to gravity, I hear something. Something that sounds awfully like a car. And not just any car: Frank's car. I'm afraid to look, because what if my ears are playing tricks on me? I wait until the sound gets louder and then when I finally look up, Frank's practically on top of me and I have to run to where he's pulled over so he doesn't leave without me. But it turns out there's no chance of that since he's turned the motor off. Which is weird, because usually he keeps the car running, I hop in, and off we go. But I'm so happy to see him, I don't even care. I just run around to my side of the car and yank open the door. Only it doesn't yank. I try again and practically pull my arm out of its socket before it finally dawns on me that the door is locked.

What gives? I knock on the window but Frank ignores me. I bend down to look through the glass and see he's just staring out the windshield straight ahead of him, like there's something really fascinating going on right in front of the car. Which there isn't.

I go around to Frank's side and rap on his window. He rolls it down without even looking at me and I know I have to wait. I look down at a gray pebble and move it around with the toe of my sneaker, because I know Frank doesn't like being stared at. After a minute he turns to me and fixes me with those gorgeous eyes of his, and then I don't dare move, like I'm a rabbit caught in a pair of headlights.

"Listen, Vanessa," Frank says, and for a split second I don't even know what he's talking about. Then I remember he thinks that's my name.

"Vanessa," Frank says again, shaking his head. "I don't know if I can see you anymore."

"Why not?" The words burst out of my mouth like I've just been sucker-punched.

"It's not that I'm not attracted to you," he says, and my heart starts pounding. "You're a very beautiful woman." He runs his tongue across his top lip and looks me up and down, letting his eyes rest on my chest for a minute until my legs go all rubbery like they did yesterday when we were fooling around.

Frank reaches through the window and touches my arm. Even through Mike's jacket and my sweater, his fingers feel hot. "Listen, babe." He lowers his voice, and I have to lean in closer. "How old are you?"

"Old enough," I say, but that doesn't cut it this time. Maybe because my voice comes out all small and shaky. Frank frowns and shifts in his seat like he's about to start the car and drive away.

"Seventeen," I blurt out, trying not to sound totally panicked, but Frank doesn't buy it. He sort of snorts and sort of laughs.

"Sixteen," I say, but the word comes out all squeaky with a question mark at the end.

Frank doesn't say anything but he gives me this look, like *Tell me the truth or else,* so I do.

"Almost sixteen," I finally confess, and then I let out this big sigh because I know he'll never want to be with me now that it's out in the open that I'm just a kid.

"See, Vanessa," Frank says, and every time he says my name, my secret name that only the two of us know, I ooze with happiness. "I could get in big trouble for seeing you." He pauses to let his words sink in. "Some people out there"—Frank takes his arm off my sleeve and makes a sweeping gesture—"wouldn't understand about us."

"I won't tell anyone, Frank. You know that. I could get in trouble too." While I'm saying this, I'm thinking, *Please, please put your hand back on my arm.*

"What could they do to you? Ground you for a month? Take away your TV privileges?" Frank sounds totally disgusted, like I'm only three years old. "I could get in major hot water for being with you, little girl." He pulls a cigarette out of the pack of Marlboros on his dashboard and taps it on my arm. "It's not for nothing they call sweet things like you jailbait."

"What?" I'm only half listening to Frank because I'm concentrating so hard on trying to will him to put his hand back on my arm. Frank shakes his head like I'm the dumbest person on the planet. Then he lights his cigarette and blows a long stream of smoke in my face, which is completely rude, but I know he doesn't do it on purpose.

"Vanessa," Frank says, soft as a kiss, like I'm something he misses already even though I'm standing right there in front of him. "This is a really screwed-up world, sweetheart. A lot of people wouldn't understand about us. Haven't you ever heard of statutory rape?"

"What?" I say again. I'm floating on the soft cloud of the word *sweetheart* and then I land on my butt hard, with the thunk of the word *rape*. Rape? He's got to be kidding. I take a step back because I feel off balance, like the world is spinning too fast.

"Frank, what are you talking about?" My voice comes out as a whisper. "Of course I've heard of statutory rape, but you would never rape me. You'd never force me to do anything. I know you wouldn't." I have to convince him somehow that everything's all right. "Frank," I say, my voice a little louder. "First of all, no one's going to find out about us. And second of all, I'm not a baby. I'm making my own choices. And I'm choosing to be with you. I like being with you."

"Why?"

"Why?" What does he mean, why? "Because, I don't know, you make me feel good."

"How?"

"Frank, you know how."

"Vanessa, if I knew I wouldn't be asking you."

God, sometimes Frank is so annoying. Do I have to spell it out for him? "You make me feel good by, you know. When we're together." My voice drops down to a whisper again and I feel my face get all hot and red, so I look down at my sneakers, hoping I won't cry. I don't even know why I'm so upset. But I am.

I wait for Frank to say something else but he just puffs away on his cigarette until he gets down to the filter and then he pitches it out the window. God, I hate that. I want to run over and step on his butt with my sneaker and then pocket it but of course I don't. I just stand there trying not to cry because I know this is the end and I'm sure Frank knows it too, so why doesn't he just say it already so I can go home and kill myself?

But when Frank finally does speak, he doesn't say good-bye. He says, "Get in," and before I can even say, *what?* he's leaning across the front seat to unlock my door and I'm so happy I do start to cry, which is really weird because who cries when they're happy unless they're completely insane?

I run around to my side of the car and get in quick before Frank changes his mind. I turn toward him but he's staring out the window again with this vague expression on his face. He doesn't move for a long time. I look at the screwdriver on the dashboard and think, *Pick it up, Frank. Start the car.* But he doesn't.

Finally, when I just can't stand it anymore, I say, "Aren't we going?" but Frank doesn't bother to answer my question, and why should he? Isn't it obvious we're not going anywhere?

"Listen, Vanessa." When Frank finally does talk, I jump a little and he calms me down by putting his hand on my thigh. "I want you to do something for me."

"What?" I say, but what I'm thinking is *You name it, Frank. Your wish is my command.*

"I want you . . ." Frank pauses, and while he's thinking, his hand works its way up to my jacket. Then his hand is under my jacket. Then it's under my sweater.

"What is it?" I whisper, since I can hardly breathe.

"Since I'm taking such a big risk to be with you, you have to take a big risk too." As he talks to me, his hand moves softly and I start to feel sleepy, as if Frank were hypnotizing me.

"I want you to give me something that's really important to you. Something that will show me we're in this together."

"Here." I pull away from Frank long enough to reach into my pocket, grab my lucky shell, and offer it to him.

"What's that?"

"A shell."

"A shell?" He says the word *shell* like he's never heard it before.

"Yeah, take it." I give it to him and he turns it over on his palm. "It's my lucky shell. My brother gave it to me."

"A shell." Frank blows air out of the right side of his mouth like now he's heard everything. "A shell, huh. That's just kid stuff." Frank pokes my shell with his finger like it might be alive or something, and then he chucks it out the window.

"Frank!" Oh my God, is he nuts? What if some stupid Buick comes along and runs over my shell? My special shell that probably got tossed around the ocean for over a billion years before Mike found it. And then for it to wind up being crushed to death by some housewife on her way to the butcher to pick up a pot roast just doesn't seem fair. I want to run out of the car and grab it right now but I don't dare.

"Something you could get in a lot of trouble for,"

Frank says, sneaking his hand up under my clothes again and going on like nothing's even happened. And in one second I've got it. I'll bring him Shirley's wedding ring. She'll never miss it. She doesn't even wear it anymore since she likes the twenty-diamond anniversary band Fred gave her so much better.

"I know what I can bring you," I say, sounding like I'm in a big hurry to race out of the car and get it. Even though Frank's hand feels nice and everything, I'm frantic to get out of there on account of my shell. I can see it on the side of the road, an accident waiting to happen. "I'll bring it tomorrow, okay?"

"Tomorrow," Frank says, giving me an extra squeeze before taking his hand away. I know that's my cue to get out of the car, so I do. Frank starts the ignition and drives off, with the usual wave and smile. He heads straight for my shell and my whole body stiffens waiting to hear that awful crunch, but at the last minute Frank swerves the other way. See, he's not really mean, he just likes to tease me. I run over and pick up my shell.

"There, see," I say to it, "everything's okay. You're not hurt. That was a little scary, but you're all right now. You're all right." I lick my finger and clean the dust off my shell before I put it back in my pocket where it's nice and safe. Then I hurry home like a girl with a mission. Which is exactly what I am.

SIX

Nuts. Wouldn't you know it? I was hoping Shirley would be out at her figure salon or at the mall or playing bridge with some of her friends or something, but no such luck. Nope, I know she's definitely home since her big boat of a car is taking up our whole stupid driveway. Oh, this is great, just great. Now what am I supposed to do?

After I let myself in—remembering to shut off the burglar alarm this time—I hang up my coat and put on this big sweater I keep in the hall closet, because it's pretty chilly in here. Ever since Shirley started going through the Change she's been hot all the time so she keeps the heat on low. Before this, she was a total Ice

Queen. She complained about being cold so much that last year Mike and I bought her electric socks for her birthday, which actually worked (they ran on batteries). But now she's too hot to wear them. Figures. The one time we did anything right.

"Is that you, Andrea?" Shirley yells her usual greeting from the den.

Who does she think it is, Alice in Wonderland? "Yeah," I yell back. "It's me."

"Can you make me a cup of coffee, please?"

Without bothering to answer, I shuffle into the kitchen, turn on the flame under the teakettle, and dump a teaspoon of instant Maxwell House coffee into a mug. Then I tear open a pink packet of Sweet'n Low and dump that in too. After the teakettle whistles, I add the boiling water along with a little skim milk and bring Shirley's drink into the den.

"Voilà," I say with a little bow.

Shirley turns away from *General Hospital* and frowns instantly. "Andrea," she says, "didn't you wear that outfit yesterday?"

I study the patched dungarees and black pullover I'm wearing under my floppy sweater and shrug. "Maybe."

"Maybe? What do you mean maybe? Don't you know?"

I shrug again. "Not really."

Shirley shakes her head and takes a sip of her coffee. "Andrea, personal hygiene is very important. I've told you that a million times. You don't think boys notice these things, but they do."

Yeah, yeah, yeah, I think, and I guess Shirley notices I'm not listening because she stops her tirade and asks, "How was school?"

"Fine." I mean, what am I supposed to tell her? My classes were totally boring, I ate lunch by myself as usual, and Donald Caruso called me a *dee*-mented dyke? And I'm certainly not going to tell her about my extra-curricular activities. "What did you do today?" I ask, not that I really care, but it's a good way to take the focus off me.

"I played mah-jongg at Mrs. Oppenheim's house," Shirley says, lighting a cigarette. "And she made the most interesting lunch. She used a wok—you know, that big round pan they use at Chinese restaurants—and she made her own duck sauce and . . . "

For someone who's constantly trying to lose weight, Shirley is sure obsessed with eating. I try not to fall asleep as she lists every ingredient Mrs. Oppenheim used in her Oriental stir-fry, but I can only take so much, so finally I blurt out while Shirley's still talking, "May I please be excused?"

Shirley's bottom lip curls and I know she's considering scolding me for my rudeness, but she just says, "All right, Andrea. There's a load of laundry in the basket sitting on the washing machine. Would you mind putting it away for me?"

"Surely, Shirley," I say in my usual surly way so I won't sound too eager. Under normal circumstances I would mind, but today is anything but normal. And this is great—laundry patrol gives me access to the entire house, and I do have a mission to accomplish.

I get the basket of clothes from the laundry room, take it upstairs, dump it out on Fred and Shirley's bed, and start sorting. If you really think about it—and I try not to—it's gross that I have to touch the Parental Units' underwear. Thank God Shirley's a total fanatic about detergent and bleach, so everything is white as snow. But still, these pieces of cotton have been right up against certain parts of the human body that I'd prefer not to think about. Not that Fred and Shirley ever have sex anymore. Though, don't get me wrong, I'm not stupid enough to think they only did it twice and Mike and I were the result. Or three times, really, if you count my older sister.

You're probably wondering why I never mentioned my older sister before. Well, I never met her, so I don't really know what to say about her. She died before I was born. In a car crash. She was one and a half. Fred and Shirley never told me about her, but Mike did.

See, they were all living in the city then, the Units along with my sister, who was just a baby, and Mike, who was five at the time, and then one summer they rented a car to go to the Catskills for a vacation. They drove along for hours and hours and everyone was just fine until they were almost there and then for some reason my sister started bawling her head off. Shirley tried singing to her, giving her a bottle, a toy, a cookie, but nothing worked, so finally she took her from the backseat up to the front and held her on her lap. It seemed safe enough because they weren't on the highway anymore; they were driving through a bunch of dinky little towns and not going all that fast. But still, Shirley should have known better.

There's a reason why they call where she was sitting the suicide seat.

Anyway, just as they got to the town they were going to, this drunk ran a red light and plowed right into Shirley's side of the car and the baby went flying and that was that. Mike didn't get hurt much, and Fred was basically okay too. Shirley was kind of cut up and bruised and I think maybe she broke something, but she wasn't in critical condition or anything. Even the guy who smashed into them didn't get hurt too badly. But the baby flew right through the window.

Her name was Melissa. Melissa Amy Kaplan. You wouldn't think she'd be a secret, but she is, I don't know why. I guess talking about her makes Shirley too sad. We don't even have any pictures of her around the house or anything; they're all tucked away in this box Shirley keeps on the top shelf of her closet. I discovered it once when I was putting away laundry like I'm doing now. That's how I found out about her. I saw all these pictures of Shirley holding a baby girl who wasn't me, so I asked Mike about it.

Thinking about all this makes me want to look at Shirley's old pictures again, so I go into her closet and take the box down from the shelf. I stay in the closet with it, though, in case Shirley decides to come upstairs.

The box smells musty and the pictures are all just thrown in, not sorted or anything. I flip through a few and then come to a close-up of Melissa sitting in her high chair. She is really cute, I have to admit, and just the opposite of me: Melissa had straight hair; mine is curly.

Melissa was pretty and petite; I am plain, not to mention pleasingly plump. According to Mike, Melissa hardly cried, and I was the original Miss Colic of Suffolk County. Melissa was always happy, I guess, and I'm not exactly the most cheerful person on the planet.

If it wasn't for the accident, I wouldn't even be here. Mike says after it happened, Shirley became a completely different person overnight. He says Shirley was always happy before, and she used to sing all the time, which is completely impossible to imagine. Though in these pictures, she does look a lot happier than I've ever seen her. Like in this one, she's smiling and holding Melissa on her lap. And here's another one with her and baby Mike, both of them laughing with their heads thrown back. There's only one or two pictures of me in here. Once I asked Shirley why she has hardly any baby pictures of me around the house and she said that with two kids to run after, there wasn't any time for photos. But clearly there was plenty of time when it was Mike and Melissa instead of Mike and me.

Anyway, Mike says Shirley got really depressed after the accident because she thought that it was all her fault since she's the one who unbuckled the baby and put her on her lap. I guess she even felt suicidal for a while, but she refused to see a shrink like Fred wanted her to. She just went to her regular doctor and got a lifetime supply of Valium, which she still takes—I've seen the vial in her purse—not that they seem to help.

So finally, the doctor said the only thing that would get Shirley undepressed would be to have another baby.

So I guess she and Fred went at it, because here I am. But—surprise, surprise—even my arrival didn't cheer old Shirley up. My theory is that somewhere deep inside Shirley's mind, she thought she and Fred were making another little Melissa. They even planned it so we'd have the same birthday and everything, and we almost do; mine's December 17 and hers was December 12. But in all other ways, I think Shirley would say I'm nothing but one great big fat disappointment.

God, this is depressing. *Snap out of it, Andi,* I tell myself. *You've got a job to do.* And I'm not talking about the wash.

I put the pictures back, slide the box up onto its shelf, and go back to sorting clothes. When everything's folded, I bring a pile of Shirley's underwear and bras over to her dresser, put it away, and then feel around for the little brown velvet box she keeps her ring in. If Shirley knew I was going to give this to Frank, she'd kill me, but she'll never miss it. It's always in the same exact spot, under this black garter belt and matching bra she never wears. At least, I don't think she ever wears them; they never show up in the wash.

When I'm done putting the clothes away, I pocket Shirley's ring and head for Mike's room. I like hanging out in here sometimes, I don't know why. Mike took most of his stuff off to college so there's hardly anything left except his bed, his empty dresser, and his desk, which has old papers like his junior high report cards and stuff crammed into the middle drawer. There's still a few things in his closet too, like this beat-up tan trench coat and a pair of old rubber boots I'm sure Mike wouldn't be caught dead in up at college.

I lie down on Mike's bed and stare up at the ceiling. One thing my brother couldn't take with him to college are the glow-in-the-dark stars that Fred pasted up for him. When Mike was little, he said he wanted to be an "outer-space guy" (as opposed to the spaced-out guy he turned out to be) so Fred glued all these glow-in-the-dark stars up on his ceiling in the shape of constellations like the Big Dipper and Orion. Mike also has these cool op-art posters on the wall that glow in the dark when you put his special black light on. Plus he has a beanbag chair and a Lava lamp. He wanted to get a water bed, too, but Shirley and Fred put their foot down over that one.

Anyway, lying here on Mike's bed makes me wish I could talk to him, but I'm not allowed to make any long-distance calls until after five o'clock, when the rates go down. And anyway, last time we spoke on the phone, Mike wasn't exactly coherent. I barely said hello before he started ranting and raving about this new poem he was writing called "Yowl."

"It's just like that famous poem 'Howl,'" Mike said.

"'Howl'?" I asked.

"Yeah, you know, 'Howl,' by Allen Ginsberg?"

"Allen who?"

"Allen Ginsberg? The beat poet? Only the greatest bard since Shakespeare, Squirt. Sheesh, don't they teach you anything at that school I had to mortgage my teeth to send you to?" Mike asked, which is what Fred is always saying to him. "So listen to this, okay? Ginsberg's poem starts off, 'I saw the best minds of my generation . . . ,' so my poem starts off, 'I saw the best *spines* of my generation. . . .' Get it, Squirt?"

"Uh, not really."

"*Spines,* Squirt. You know, backbone. As in strength. As in standing up for what you believe in."

"Uh, sure, Mike. Whatever."

"Just listen," Mike said, and then he proceeded to recite this extremely long poem that didn't exactly sound brilliant to me. I don't know if he was reading his poem or Allen Ginsberg's poem, but whichever one it was, it didn't make a whole lot of sense. In the middle of all this, I heard a click, which meant that Fred had picked up the upstairs extension like he sometimes does when Mike and I are on the phone. Sure enough, two seconds later Fred started screaming about how much this call was costing him and then we hung up.

After a while hanging out in Mike's room gets boring, so I go into my own room, sit down at my desk, and take out Shirley's ring. The box she keeps it in feels as soft as Bessie's back, and when I open the cover the hinges squeak. Inside, the box is lined with white satin and there's a little slit where the ring sits. The ring is shiny and simple, and inside it's engraved *F.K. to S.K. forever,* which was a surprise from Fred to Shirley the day they tied the knot. Though in my opinion, tied the noose is more like it.

I take the ring out of the box and slip it on my ring finger. It gets stuck above my second knuckle, so I switch it to my pinkie, where it fits better, but still it's kind of tight. I could probably force it all the way down but I don't because what if I can't get it off?

Just as I slide the ring off my pinkie I hear footsteps coming up the stairs, so I shove the ring back in its box, close the lid, which makes this really loud crack, and jam the whole thing back in my pocket. I don't know why I'm so jumpy; it's not like Shirley ever comes in here or anything. After a few minutes I hear the toilet flushing, then Shirley's footsteps going down the stairs, and I let out my breath, which I didn't even know I was holding. *God, Andi, calm down,* I tell myself. I take a few deep breaths and then put Shirley's ring in my knapsack to bring to Frank tomorrow. I know I shouldn't do it—it *is* my own mother's wedding ring and everything—but Frank said I had to take a big risk and he's right, because look what he's risking for me: *everything.* He must really like me. I mean, really, *really* like me. I can't believe he could go to jail for making out with me. Give me a break. It's not like he put a gun to my head and forced me to do anything. Frank would never do that. And besides, I want to be with him. More than I've ever wanted any-thing in my whole entire life. So what else could I bring the guy to show I'm serious about him? Nothing.

Still, the whole thing makes me kind of nervous, so I check around my room to see if I can bring Frank some-thing else instead. Nothing in my closet but clothes, most of which don't even fit. Nothing on my bookshelf but all my animal books, plus other books like *Little Women* and *Huckleberry Finn,* which we had to read for school. Nothing on my bed but stuffed animals. Nothing too interesting in my jewelry box except a Jewish star from my grandmother which I never wear, and the gold name necklace that Fred and Shirley gave me for my thirteenth birthday, which I never wear either. And this braided leather bracelet that Ronnie gave me before she left. I gave her one too, and I wonder if she still has it. Not that I really care.

Anyway, I'm sure Frank would just think all this is kid stuff as opposed to Shirley's ring, which I bet is fourteen-carat gold, which means it's got to be worth something. And I'm sure I won't get caught stealing it, either. I'm not even stealing it, really, just borrowing it. And besides that, Frank and I aren't doing anything wrong. What kind of idiotic world is this anyway, where two people have to worry so much when all they really want to do is be together and fall in love?

SEVEN

Bring me her broomstick. . . . **That's what this feels like:** Frank's the Wizard of Oz, I'm Dorothy Gale from Kansas, and Shirley's the Wicked Witch of the West. All day long, Shirley's wedding ring has been burning a hole in my pocket. When I got to school this morning, I thought about putting it in my locker, but what if some stupid kid called in a bomb scare like Donald Caruso did last week when he didn't study for his math test? We all knew it was him because while everyone was standing outside waiting for the all-clear bell to ring, it began to rain and Donna Rizzo started screaming at Donald, "Now look what you've done. This sweater is ruined. Ruined!" And then she stomped off with Donald trotting behind her. Anyway, the point is we get bomb scares at least once a week and the fire department has to come and search the entire building, including our lockers, and what would happen if I got caught? That would not be pretty.

God, this day is taking forever. I can't pay attention to anything my teachers are saying because all I want to do is get out of here and see the expression on Frank's face when I give him Shirley's ring.

As soon as school is over, I grab my coat from my locker and hurry away before Donald Caruso can try and stop me. The big idiot just loves to pop my cork at the end of the day.

"Hey, Dee-Dee," he calls, "what's your hurry? C'mere, I want to *dee*-scuss something with you."

Blow me, I think, but of course I don't say it. I just keep going.

"What's your big hurry, Dee-Dee? *She* can wait," he yells, but I don't even slow down. Donald Caruso is so stupid. As if I would ever be in this much of a hurry to meet a girl.

"Hey, Hillary." I hear Donald say behind me. "Whoa, Nellie."

Poor Hillary Jacoby, nicknamed Horseface Hillary because of her equine features, including her enormous eyes, her sunken cheeks, and her incredibly long, horselike teeth. I guess since Donald can't get a rise out of me today, he's going to give her a run for her money. I hear him behind me neighing, snorting, and pawing the ground with his big fat foot. Next to me, Hillary is Donald's favorite target, and he does really mean things to her. Once he left a jar of rubber cement in front of her locker with a note that said *See you at the glue factory.*

I hightail it out of there, and as soon as I get to Farm Hill Road I see Frank in the brown VW, right in our spot, with the motor running just like it should be. I go to my side of the car, pull on the door handle, and almost dislocate my shoulder before it sinks into my thick skull that the door is locked again. *This is really getting old,* I think as I walk around the car to Frank's side and wait for him to roll down his window.

"Hey, Frank," I say when he does, but he doesn't say anything back. He just sticks out his hand and waits until I reach into my pocket and place the brown velvet box in his palm. He keeps his face still, so I can't tell if he's disappointed or impressed. Then, just as I'm about to say, "Open it," he does. I wait a minute but he still has no reaction.

"It's my mother's wedding ring," I say, pretending he asked, *What is it?*

"What is she, a midget?" He takes the ring out of its box and examines it. It looks really tiny and lost in his big hairy hand. Then he puts it on his pinkie, his right pinkie, the one that's all disfigured, and I start feeling really jumpy, like I might start to laugh. Or cry. I just want him to take it off his pinkie, so I say, "Look inside," and reach over to grab it, but he moves his hand away so I can't reach.

"Patience, Vanessa," he says, holding his hand out in front of him, like he's a woman in a jewelry store admiring a ring she's thinking of buying. Something rises in my throat, my lunch maybe, so I swallow hard and wait. Finally, he takes it off.

"Look at the inscription," I say, pointing. "My father did that to surprise my mother the day they got married."

"Sweet," Frank says like he means it. Then he puts the ring back in its little satin slit and snaps the box shut with a loud crack. "Thanks, doll," he says, and before I can say "You're welcome," he steps on the gas pedal and takes off. Just like that.

I can't believe it. My mouth must be hanging open because all of a sudden I start coughing from the dirt the back wheels of the VW kicked up. "Frank!" I yell, like he can even hear me. What is he, crazy? I stand absolutely still and keep staring down the road like I'm in shock or something, waiting for him to come back even though I know he's not going to. I sink down to the ground like I'm wounded, like instead of Frank taking off with Shirley's wedding ring, he stole my heart. Except I can feel it pounding away in my chest like it's going to shatter into a million pieces unless I calm myself down.

I shut my eyes and take a few deep breaths. What did I do wrong now? I handed him my own mother's wedding ring, so why did he take off like that? What more does Frank want, blood? God, I feel like crying and I feel so mad I could just punch somebody. Somebody named Frank. Screw him. Who does he think he is, anyway? He's not so great. Maybe I'll just get Shirley's ring back and break up with him. Yeah, right. How can I break up with him if I never even see him again? And what about

Shirley's ring? Frank wouldn't sell it or anything, would he? God, if Frank doesn't show up tomorrow, I'll kill him, I really will. I guess I should just go home, but I don't really feel like moving. So I lean back against the fence post, pick up a strand of hair, and just rip the living daylights out of my poor split ends.

✖   ✖   ✖

Thank God it's Friday. At least I don't have to wait the entire weekend to see if I still have a boyfriend or not. When the final bell rings, I grab my coat and hurry out the door before I can bump into Donald Caruso, who I am definitely not in the mood to see today. I walk with my head down because of all things, it's raining out, so if Frank is there, my side of the car better be open—or else. And I mean it too.

I walk fast with my fists jammed in my pockets and my knapsack bouncing up and down. He just better be there, is all I have to say. And he is. And not only that, my door is open. And I don't just mean unlocked. I mean swung open wide, like a big welcome sign. Which is really stupid because now half the seat's wet on account of the rain. But it's the thought that counts, as Shirley would say, so who cares if my seat is a little damp?

I get in without saying anything because even if Frank is trying to make up, I'm still mad about yesterday. Let him say something first. And he does.

"I missed you." Frank says it so softly I can't tell if I heard it or if I just think I heard it, since it's what I want him to say.

"Really?" I ask, just to be sure.

"Really," he says, and I feel all the anger seep out of me like warm water going down a bathtub drain. He missed me!

"C'mere," Frank says, which is hard to do since the front of his car is so small and there's the stick shift between us besides. I just sort of turn toward him and he gathers me up and gives me this big hug and holds me for a minute. God, it feels so good to be with him, I don't even care that the steering wheel is digging a major hole out of my side. And then I don't mean to, but I can't help it, I start to cry.

"What's the matter?" Frank asks, stroking my hair.

"I thought you weren't coming back." I gulp for air because I'm all smushed up against his jacket. "I thought . . ." I hardly dare think it, let alone say it. ". . . I'd never see you again."

"Silly girl." Frank holds me even tighter. I love it when he's like this. "Listen, Vanessa," he says. "Relationships are built on trust. You have to trust me." He's talking quietly now, his voice all soft and soothing, the way you'd talk to a frightened animal.

"Why did you just leave yesterday?" I ask his chest.

"I had to see a man about a horse."

"What?" I sit up and look at him. "What man? What horse?"

"Vanessa, it's just an expression. I had to meet someone."

"Who?"

"None of your business."

Even though that's true, I don't let up. "Lloyd?"

"Who?"

"Lloyd, you know, your partner in crime."

"Yeah, Lloyd," Frank says, but he doesn't sound like he's telling the truth. What if he was with another girl?

"Really? It was Lloyd?"

"Vanessa, what is this, an interrogation?"

"No," I say, "but it would have been nice if you'd told me."

"And it would be nice if you trusted me," he says.

I don't say anything back, but I guess that's true.

"Let's change the subject." Frank reaches behind us into the backseat. "Look, I brought you a present."

"You did?" I couldn't be more surprised if he said *Look, will you marry me?*

"Here." Frank twists back around and hands me a box all wrapped up in red paper and tied with a shiny gold ribbon.

"What is it?" I ask. I'm so excited I can hardly stand it. I never got a present from a boy, let alone a man before.

"You'll see," he says. "Don't open it yet. Let's go kiss and make up."

"Okay," I agree, even though that's a weird thing for Frank to say since he's never kissed me. As you know, we've done other stuff, but for some reason he's never given me a big fat smackeroo. Maybe he will today.

Frank starts driving and I wish he would put his hand on my leg but he doesn't. Instead, after a few minutes, he takes *my* hand and puts it on *his* leg. And then between his legs. All I can think of is that joke: *Is that a banana in your pocket or are you just happy to see me?* Which isn't very funny.

We get to the house and Frank actually seems glad to

be with me which is nice for a change. And it's stopped raining, which I take as a good sign, even though it's too cloudy for a rainbow. Frank even holds my hand as we walk up the driveway. I'm holding my present under my right arm, so Frank has to hold my left hand with his right one and I can feel where his pinkie ends—the tip is rougher than the rest of his skin—but I try not to dwell on it because if I do, I'll definitely get grossed out.

We get to the door and when Frank lets go of my hand to open it, I blurt out without thinking, "What happened to your pinkie?" Me and my big mouth. The smile disappears from Frank's face as fast as Fred's always does the second he sees my report card.

"I cut myself," Frank says slowly.

"How? When?" The words fly out of my mouth before I can stop them. But maybe it would be better if I knew all the gory details. Then at least I wouldn't wonder anymore.

Frank studies his pinkie and then says softly, almost like he's talking to himself, "Once upon a time there was a little boy named Frankie. And Frankie was a real fifty-pound weakling. All the other kids called him sissy-boy and used him as a punching bag. So one day little Frankie decides he's had it and he's going to toughen up. So he takes the biggest kitchen knife he can find to school, and in the middle of recess, he gathers all the kids who are always torturing him in a big circle and then he sits down right in front of them and cuts the tip of his finger off. And the other kids freak, not because there's blood everywhere, but because"—and here Frank looks right up at me and there's something in his eyes I've never seen before—"because, Vanessa, the other kids know if Frankie could do that to himself, he could do a whole lot worse to them. The End."

Frank drops his hand, opens the door to the house, and goes inside without waiting for me, like he doesn't care if I follow or not. I scurry after him, with Shirley's voice ringing in my ear, *There, Andrea, are you happy now?* I can't believe I ruined a perfectly good afternoon by being so nosy and rude.

"Frank, I'm sorry," I say, following him into the kitchen. He's already perched on the counter, fishing for a cigarette.

"Aren't you going to open your present?" he asks, like he's already forgotten the whole thing.

"Sure," I say, anxious to forget it too. I don't think Frank's a liar or anything, but how could he cut his own finger like that? Didn't it hurt? What did the other kids do? And the teachers? And his parents?

"Go on." Frank motions toward the box. I shake it up and down, stalling a little, because for some reason, I'm afraid the present is going to be something gross, like the bloody tip of Frank's pinkie, or a frozen horse turd like Donald Caruso once wrapped up in a fancy box and gave to Horseface Hillary.

I pull the gold ribbon slowly, and then carefully remove the red wrapping paper and open the box. Oh my God, it's a bra. A black bra. A black lace bra. Hiding beneath this red tissue paper like something scared. I pull it out and I'm just about to say "Oh, Frank, it's beautiful," when I see something else. Black lace underwear. And some kind of flimsy black lace thing to wear on top of it.

"Put it on," Frank says in a hoarse voice that sounds like he has a bad cold or just woke up from a nap. I don't know how I feel about this exactly, but I also know that how I feel doesn't matter. And anyway, guys are supposed to like this sort of stuff, and I want to make Frank happy, don't I?

At least Frank turns his back while I change my clothes. I hear him light a cigarette while I take off Mike's jacket and the strike of the match startles me for a second, it's so spooky and quiet in here. I pick up my new bra and study it for a minute. It's a 38D, which just happens to fit me perfectly. How did Frank know? It's kind of weird but then again, not surprising. For some reason, I have a funny feeling there are lots of things about me that Frank already knows.

When I finish putting on Frank's present, I just stand there waiting and feeling totally self-conscious. I've never worn lingerie before and I wonder what I look like. I guess I'll never know since there's no mirror in here, which is probably just as well, because as Shirley always says, what you don't know can't hurt you.

Frank must hear that I'm not fidgeting anymore because he turns around and motions to me. "C'mere, baby," he says, and I take a step toward him. "Beautiful," he says quietly, like he's talking more to himself than to me. The cigarette in his mouth moves up and down with the word. "Beautiful," he says again, like I'm a painting he just finished. "You look like a movie star, you know that, Vanessa?" He smiles and studies me with his head cocked to one side like he's an artist and I'm his model. I half expect him to raise his thumb and close one eye, but of course he doesn't. "Black suits you," he says, and I think, *Tell that to Shirley.* I just watch Frank watching me. His eyes change as he looks at me. They get bigger and darker, and his face softens. I like having this effect on someone. Though what the effect is I'm not exactly sure.

"Come closer—I won't bite," Frank says, and I go to him and let him touch me. That's when I forget everything: school, stupid Donald Caruso, my parents . . . I just float away and let Frank go further than he did last time. But I don't mind. Lots of girls at my school have gone to third base and even further, and they've done it with stupid teenage boys, not someone as mature and wonderful as Frank.

When Frank is done he gathers me up in his arms and rocks me. I like sitting on his lap. I feel all cozy and loved and safe. After a while he turns me around so he can look at me and says, his liquid brown eyes all dark and serious, "Thank you, Vanessa."

"For what?"

"For being so beautiful. And for spending time with me."

I can't believe my ears. I mean, if anything, I should be thanking him.

"You're really special, Vanessa." Frank runs his finger all the way from my forehead down to my cheek to my neck to my throat. "You're not like other girls your age.

You really know how to make a man happy. We're going to have lots of good times together." Frank gathers me close again and starts rocking me. "I knew the minute I saw you, you were different than other girls. Most high school girls aren't very smart, but you're like a grown woman. You're much more mature. You know what's important in life. You and me, baby, we're cut from the same cloth."

No one's ever said so many nice things to me before. I lean into Frank but stay a little on guard because I know he can change like the weather: sunny one minute, stormy the next.

"Sit back and relax a minute, sweetheart." Frank adjusts us so I'm all the way up on his lap. "I'll miss you this weekend," Frank croons while he hugs me tight, and it feels really nice. But then he snaps out of it and jerks up and pushes me away.

"What happened?" I ask. "Did I hurt you? Am I too heavy?"

Frank doesn't answer. He's up on his feet already and I feel like a total moron just sitting on the cold floor practically naked except for this flimsy black lace.

"Get dressed," Frank says in his voice that lets me know he's done with me. I scramble to my feet and throw on my clothes, trying not to think about anything, because if I do, I'll cry. I shrug on Mike's jacket and follow Frank down the stairs, out of the house, and into the car without a word. I don't know why he's mad at me again and I wish he'd tell me but he doesn't and I know it's not a good idea to ask. Maybe he thinks I'm selfish. He spent all that time making me feel good and I didn't do anything for him. Maybe I should do something right now, like reach over and touch him while he's driving, but I don't know, that could get kind of dangerous. And anyway, Frank's always the one who makes the first move.

We don't say anything the whole way back to where he drops me off, and then before I know it we've arrived, and there's nothing for me to do but get out of the car. I want Frank to say something, anything, but he doesn't. I try to think of something to say, but all I can come up with is *Thanks a lot,* or *Have a great weekend,* which both sound completely lame. So I just wave and watch him drive off and pray the weekend will fly by until I get to see him Monday, after school.

EIGHT

Everything's so different now that I have a reason to get up in the morning. I'm standing here in the kitchen making Fred's dinner, and I'm actually *humming,* and I'm not exactly the humming type. But can you believe it—*I've* had a boyfriend for more than a month. Me, Andrea Robin Kaplan, the loser no one will eat lunch with, the klutz nobody picks to be on their softball team during gym, the big fat slob whose thighs rub together in the summer because her shorts are too tight. And not just any boyfriend either. I'm not talking about some pimply-faced, greasy-haired, stupid kid with braces as long as the entire Long Island Rail Road strung across his teeth. I'm talking about a grown-up *man.*

I wish I were standing here making Frank's supper instead of Fred's, but that's the way it goes, I guess. Shirley's the one who should really be preparing Fred's chow, but Shirley spends as little time as possible in the kitchen these days. She says it's too tempting to be around all that food and God forbid she should eat something she thinks she's not supposed to—she might gain an ounce or two. You'd think she'd tell me to stay out of the kitchen too, since according to her I'm the one who needs to lose weight, but hey, someone has to cook Freddie Boy his dinner; he's certainly not going to do it himself.

So what happens nowadays is Shirley defrosts something during the day—lamb chops, a chicken breast, whatever—and then it's my job to cook the carcass she's left out on the counter. Tonight it's a T-bone steak, which is at least easy to make. I put on a pair of oversized black oven mitts so I don't touch the meat with my bare hands, slit open the cellophane package with a knife, plop the steak onto a flat metal pan, and put it in the oven to broil. It's totally unfair that I have to cook Fred's suppers, especially since he eats meat every night and I'm a vegetarian, but when I complained to Shirley about it, she said, "Andrea, life isn't fair," which is basically her answer to everything.

I sit down at the kitchen table while Fred's steak is cooking, stare out the window, and think about—what else?—me and Frank. We've come a long way in the past few weeks and I can't even believe how happy I am. Frank and I are just perfect for each other. That's because, as Frank told me, girls and boys mature at different rates, which was hardly news to me. It's a biological thing, really. See, as soon as a girl gets her period, she's sexually mature, which usually happens when she's eleven or twelve (I was ten), and boys that age haven't even started shaving yet. That's why older men and younger women go so well together. Frank says since girls mature twice as fast as boys, a man should be at least twice as old as his girlfriend.

Frank is different than anyone I've ever met before. He treats me like a grown-up, not like a kid. Like, if we have problems, which we do, like any other couple, we talk things through and work them out. Take that Friday a few weeks ago, for example, the day he gave me the black outfit. First we were having a great time, and then when we had to leave, Frank got nasty. The next time I saw him, I told him he had hurt my feelings. He apologized and explained that he gets a little distant at the end of our time together because it's so hard for him to leave me and not see me again for an entire day. So who can blame him for getting cranky at the end of our visits?

And anyway, after school when he picks me up he's always happy to see me, and lots of times he brings me presents. He got me a red lace outfit just like the black one, and he also bought me a few dresses, including a waitress's uniform and a French maid's outfit, which are both short, low-cut, and very tight.

At first I was completely embarrassed about putting on all this stuff, but Frank said I was being ridiculous and that I have a perfect figure. Nice and curvy. Voluptuous. He says I'm built exactly the way a woman should be. (I wish he could tell that to Shirley.) Plus he brings me all kinds of things he says are essential to a woman's wardrobe: garter belts and fishnet stockings and high-heeled shoes. I never really liked playing dress-up before, but I don't know, it's different with Frank.

Since obviously I can't bring all the stuff Frank gives me home, I keep everything at the house we go to. I use one room as a dressing room and put all the stuff on the floor in the closet. When we get there, I go upstairs and put on an outfit and then come out and surprise Frank. It works pretty well, and anyway, where else am I supposed to keep all my stuff? Here? Can you imagine what Shirley and Fred would say if they found it?

Not that the Rents care what I do with myself after school. I tell them, if they even ask, that I'm at the library, and as long as I get home in time to give old Freddie Boy his supper, that's all that seems to matter.

And speaking of Freddie Boy's supper, I better finish making it. I take out a box of Uncle Ben's Converted Rice (which Mike and I call Uncle Ben's Perverted Rice) and put a pot of water on to boil, even though Shirley thinks Fred should skip the starch and lose a few pounds. Then I turn his steak over, dump a can of corn into a saucepan, and add a pat of butter and a little salt. Not exactly a gourmet meal, but we're not exactly a gourmet family, in case you haven't noticed. While all this is cooking, I ignore the signs posted on the refrigerator for my benefit—SLENDERNESS IS NEXT TO GODLINESS and A MINUTE ON THE LIPS, FOREVER ON THE HIPS—and make myself a peanut butter, jelly, and banana sandwich. Not a great supper, I know, but it's the best I can do. Ever since Mike left for college, family mealtime has fallen apart around here.

I set the table, put a lid on the pot of corn, and check on the rice, and just as I'm pouring some ginger ale into a Daffy Duck glass for Fred, I hear the front door open.

"Hell-o-o-o," Fred sings from the hallway. No one bothers answering him, so he goes into the den to say hi to Shirley and then he comes into the kitchen and plops down at the table.

"What's cookin', cookie?" he asks as he loosens his tie. That's how he greets me every night.

"Steak, corn, and rice," I answer, setting his plate down in front of him. "Need anything else?" I ask, hoping to be dismissed.

"Sit down," Fred says, pulling out an empty chair next to him so I have no choice but to sit right beside him. Just my luck. Fred hates eating alone, and it's up to yours truly to keep him company. You'd think Shirley would do it—after all, she's the one who's married to the guy—but when it comes to wifely duties, Shirley can't be bothered.

"Boy, did I have a long day today," Fred says, chewing a huge hunk of steak with his mouth wide open. "I'll tell you something, there are three things in life you can always count on: death, taxes, and cavities. No one has time to pick up a toothbrush anymore. Oh well. More business for me." He takes a long gulp of ginger ale and I scrape back my chair and get up to pour him some more. While I'm away from the table, Fred pulls my chair even closer so when I sit down again, our legs are practically touching.

"Hey, guess who came in to have her teeth cleaned today?" Fred asks, like I care. He pauses and waits for me to guess. I just shrug. "Mrs. Pierson, isn't that something?"

Fred expects me to be impressed because Mrs. Pierson is the closest thing we have to a celebrity around here. She's an artist, and some of her paintings have won prizes and been in museums in New York City and everything.

"She makes a mint on those pictures of hers," Fred says, shaking his head. "I can't get over it. A couple grand for one little painting. That's not bad for a girl."

Can you believe him? I want to say, *Oh, puh-leeze, Freddie Boy. Wake up and smell the coffee. It's the seventies, for God's sake. Mrs. Pierson is a woman, not a girl. She's like forty-five years old.* But of course I don't say that. I also don't tell Fred that a lot of kids make phony phone calls to Mrs. Pierson's house because—get this—her first name is Gay. In fact, just last week I heard Donald Caruso—who else?—at the pay phone outside the cafeteria saying, "Is this Mr. Pierson? Hey, is your wife Gay? Really? Then why'd you marry her?"

"Got any more corn?" Fred asks, so I take his dish over to the stove to serve him some. I put his plate back on the table and head for the doorway, trying to give him the message that as far as I'm concerned, my job here is done, but dear old Dad doesn't see it that way.

"Sit down," Fred says, and when I slump into my chair, he pats my knee. "That was a very good dinner," he says, and then belches. Gross. He takes a sip of ginger ale, wipes his mouth with the back of his hand, and clears his throat. "So what's going on with my favorite teenage daughter?" he asks, which is supposed to be a joke, since I'm his only teenage daughter. "How's school?"

"Fine."

"How are your classes?"

"All right."

"How's your social life?" Translation: what's new in the B-O-Y department?

"It's okay," I say, which for once in my life is actually true.

"That's good." Fred lifts his steak knife, starts picking his teeth with it, and then stops. "What's that?" He points the tip of his knife toward my chin.

"What's what?"

"That." He narrows his eyes behind his glasses. "Looks like a pimple."

Oh great. My hand flies up to my face but Fred moves it away. "Don't pick it, that'll only make it worse," he says. "Maybe you should put some Clearasil on it."

Maybe you should stick to being a dentist instead of a dermatologist, I want to tell him, but I change the subject instead. "Talked to Mike lately?" I ask.

"Your brother." Fred shakes his head. "I hope he straightens himself out this time. He's never going to get into med school with the grades he's been getting."

"Med school?" I almost laugh out loud. "I don't think Mike wants to be a doctor."

"What he wants isn't the issue here," Fred says. "Your brother is very smart, if he'd only apply himself. He has a knack for science, always has."

"I think he wants to be a writer," I say, not daring to use the word *poet*.

Fred laughs. "A writer? How will he support himself doing that? What'll he live on? He'll have to eat his own words." Fred cracks up, impressed with his own cleverness. Then he pushes himself back from the table and pats his big belly. "I'm going inside to watch TV. Coming?"

"No thanks." I stand up and make myself busy gathering his dirty dishes. "I have to clean up, and then I have a ton of homework to do."

Fred lingers in the kitchen a little longer, going through the mail, glancing at the newspaper, rummaging around the junk drawer for a book of matches to light his after-dinner cigarette. Finally he goes into the den to join Shirley for their nightly smoke-out. He used to get on my case for not joining them after dinner for "family time" but I told him I have too much homework to do, and since he thinks good grades are more important than anything, he couldn't exactly argue with me. So that was the end of that, except he insists I come into the den at some point to give him and Shirley a kiss goodnight.

I rinse off Fred's dishes, load them into the dishwasher, sweep the floor, and then sit down with the newspaper before I go upstairs. I like reading the paper in the kitchen, where it's nice and quiet, even though it's pretty much the same every day—murders, robberies, and rapes, with a few recipes and fashion tips thrown in.

Frank says people like their daily routine—it gives them something to depend on, something they can count on. And I can definitely count on him. He's always right there in our spot every day after school and then away we go. Frank hasn't missed one single day except for that time when I gave him Shirley's ring, which he promises he'll give back to me the day I turn seventeen and I'm not jailbait anymore.

I turn to the entertainment section of the newspaper to check out what movies are playing, not that Frank and I could ever go to one. If we could, I'd make him take me to see some really romantic movie like *Love Story* and then go out for a pizza or maybe hot-fudge sundaes. Hey, here's an idea: we could even double-date with his friend Lloyd. It would be nice to meet one of Frank's friends, and I'm sure he'd never squeal on us.

But even I know all this is just wishful thinking, because Frank's really strict about us not being seen together in public. "Listen, Vanessa," he says, "if anyone ever found out about us, they'd throw me in jail and then I'd probably kill myself because I'd never get to see you again." See, that's what's so great about Frank. Most guys would probably say, "They'd throw me in jail and I'd kill you for telling," but Frank's not like that. He would never hurt me. He treats me like a queen.

I give up reading the paper, shut my eyes, and think about Frank and me. Everything's been going really great except there's one thing that's bothering me: we haven't gone all the way yet. Usually with couples, it's the guy pressuring the girl all the time, but with us, it's just the opposite. I want to make Frank feel as good as he makes me feel, but every time I bring it up, Frank just says, "Don't worry about me. You're the one who matters."

But you know, my birthday's coming up soon and I'm going to tell Frank. And then when he asks me what I want, I'm going to tell him I don't want him to give me something, *I* want to give *him* something. Like this Indian tribe we learned about in school once. Whenever anyone had a birthday, that person gave all their friends presents instead of the other way around. I think that's kind of cool. And wouldn't giving Frank my virginity be the best present of all? That'll really show him I love him, in case he doesn't already know. Or better yet, when he asks me what I want for my birthday, I'll wink and say, "You know," in a way that will let him know exactly what I mean. I really, really, really want to make Frank happy, and that's what every guy wants, isn't it? And once I give him that, I'm sure we'll be bound together forever.

NINE

I can't believe I overslept today. It's so unlike me, but I was having this great dream about me and Frank. We were driving somewhere in a red convertible and I had this cute little brown dog with pointy ears on my lap, and there was a breeze blowing all my hair back away from my face and all my dog's fur away from her face, and I was really, really happy. So who can blame me for not wanting to get out of bed?

But finally I drag myself out of dreamland, get dressed, and go downstairs, and guess who's there? Fred, of all people, who's moving slower than usual this morning too. That was surprise number one. And surprise number two is we're having a snowstorm. Which is strange because it's not even the middle of December yet and it doesn't usually snow much around here until the end of the month. And that drives everyone crazy because all they can think about is *Are we going to have a white Christmas? Are we going to have a white Christmas?* I mean, what's the big deal, right? I've never heard anyone ask if we're going to have a white Chanukah.

Anyway, school isn't canceled, and since I'm already running late, Fred says he'll give me a ride. Oh great. I hate being alone with my father. Last time he took me somewhere was a few Saturdays ago. "Who wants to get some ice cream?" he asked after lunch, knowing Shirley would never go—too many calories. And even though she thinks I should lose weight, Shirley told me to run along. "Go with your father," she said when Fred was out of earshot. "He needs you." I wasn't sure what that meant exactly, so I couldn't really argue. I just got in the car, and when we arrived at the restaurant, I followed my father all the way to the back. When I slid into our booth, he slid in next to me instead of across from me and sat so close I was practically pinned up against the wall. And then when the waiter came to take our order, he told him we'd split a hot-fudge sundae, even though I would have preferred my own, thank you very much. I tried not to have my spoon touch what my father's spoon had touched, but after a while it was hopeless because the ice cream and the whipped cream and the hot fudge all melted together into one great big puddle that looked like mud.

But that's all beside the point right now because after all, I do have to get to school. So when Fred's done with his coffee we go outside and he unlocks the passenger side of his Caddie to let me in. The windows are totally covered with snow and I hunch down all snuggly and safe in the front seat like a bear hibernating in a cave and watch as Fred cleans off the windshield. First all I see is his black leather glove; then I see the tan wool sleeve of his winter coat. Next his red, black, and white scarf appears, and then finally the windshield is clear and I see his fogged-up glasses and his face and the rest of the world behind him. Then Fred gets in the car and off we go. We don't talk to each other, which is fine with me, since I'm not really a morning person.

As soon as we round the corner, Fred reaches across the front seat and takes my hand in his. He's always holding my hand when we go someplace, like he's afraid if he doesn't, I'm going to float away like a helium balloon disappearing into the sky. Which, believe me, I would gladly do, if only I could. I don't really like holding Fred's hand but I put up with it because the one time I told him I didn't want to, he got all hurt and said, "What's the matter, a father can't show his own daughter some affection?" It's weird because when the three of us go somewhere, which is rare, he never holds hands with Shirley. Anyway, just because Fred holds my hand doesn't mean I have to hold his back. I just let my hand go all limp in his, like it's a dead fish, and stare out the window.

At the end of our development when we come to a

four-way stop sign, Fred brakes a little too hard and his right arm shoots out and slams across me, pinning me back against the seat for extra protection, even though I have my seat belt on. Fred keeps the car still, looking slowly to the right and to the left. "This is a very dangerous intersection," he says, like I care. "You can't be too careful." He lets two other cars go before us even though we were here first. Then he lowers his arm, takes my hand again, and holds it until he drops me off.

School passes in a blur as usual, except when it lets out, every single boy starts flinging snowballs around— first at each other and then at all the girls. Cheryl Healy and Diane Carlson start shrieking in that certain way that lets the boys know they're thrilled and terrified at the same time. Donna Rizzo is immune from the fracas because any guy knows if he even pretends to take aim at her, Donald Caruso will make mincemeat out of him in two seconds flat. And of course the big lug gets me with a freezing cold snowball at the back of the neck, but since I have Frank now, I don't really care.

I trudge past the buses and head for Farm Hill Road, and for once I really do admire the scenery. Right now Long Island looks like an old, artistic black-and-white photo. The sky is gray, the trees are black, and the snow is still pure white, like mounds of vanilla ice cream that Shirley would rather die than eat. And to make it even prettier, the snow is all twinkly, like someone scattered tiny little diamonds all over it. I know soon everything will be ruined—car exhaust will turn the snow by the side of the road all black, and dogs will lift their legs and make yellow patches—but right now it's a winter wonderland.

When I get to my spot on Farm Hill Road, I see that Frank's not here yet, but I'm probably a little early because I walked fast to keep my blood circulating so I wouldn't freeze to death. Now there's nothing to do but wait. It's too cold for Bessie to be out, which is too bad because I would have liked to talk to her. But it's just as well because Frank will be here any minute. Frank! Just thinking about him makes me shiver all over.

"Hi, Frank," I say when the Volkswagen pulls up. I get in and barely have time to close my door before we take off. Frank doesn't say hi back or anything, but I don't mind. Sometimes he says hi and sometimes he doesn't. When we first started going out, I used to take it personally, but I don't anymore because now I know that Frank's just moody. They always say women are moody, but whoever "they" are, they've never met Frank.

I glance at the backseat to see if Frank brought me a present today, but all that's back there is a flashlight, a map, and an empty Coke bottle. I'm a little disappointed, but I've got a lot of stuff at the house, so it's really okay.

We don't say much on the ride over, and then when we get to the house I go into my dressing room while Frank waits in the other upstairs room for me. It's pretty cold in the house since there's no heat, but Frank brought some down sleeping bags for us, so I know once I get in there with him it won't be so bad. Last week when I told him I was cold, he said, "Don't worry, Vanessa, I'll warm you up," and then he did, if you get the picture. Believe me, there's no lack of body heat when Frank's around.

I take off my jacket and change quickly. I put on my Lady in Red outfit, as Frank calls it: red miniskirt, red halter top, red stockings, and red shoes. Then I go into the other room, where Frank is sitting on a sleeping bag, smoking a cigarette.

"Vanessa, you look good enough to eat," Frank says in that slow way of talking that he has. I shiver a little from the cold and from being with him. I wish he'd put his arms around me—it really is freezing today—but he doesn't. Instead, he takes something out of his coat pocket.

"What's that?" I ask.

"What does it look like?" he asks back, holding it up.

"A camera." I state the obvious. "Are you going to take my picture?" I ask, my hands already making their way across my body in a futile attempt to hide my big fat stomach.

"Well, there's not much else to take pictures of in here, is there?" Frank says, waving one hand around the room. "C'mon, Vanessa, it'll be fun. And you look so good in that outfit, with your dark hair and eyes. Can't a guy have a picture of his own girlfriend?"

I'm so surprised my mouth drops open. His girl-friend? Frank's never called me his girlfriend before.

"C'mon," he says. "Put your hands down. Don't hide yourself. You're beautiful. I just want a picture or two to get me through the weekends because I miss you so much."

"All right," I say. "But promise me you won't show them to anyone."

Frank looks stunned, like I just slapped his face. "How could you even think I would do something like that?" he asks. "What we have together is so special, so sacred. Don't you trust me?"

"Of course I trust you, Frank," I say, though that's not entirely true. I mean, I do trust him, mostly. But still, I'm not thrilled at the idea of him having pictures of me in this getup. I would just die if anyone but Frank saw me like this.

"Why don't you stand over there?" Frank points to the wall.

I walk over and then, just as Frank gets ready to snap, a thought occurs to me. "Can I take some pictures of you, too?" I ask, since after all, fair is fair. And Frank's not the only one who gets lonely on the weekends.

"Vanessa"—Frank lowers the camera—"you can't go running around with pictures of me."

"But I won't show them to anyone, Frank. I promise. Don't you trust me?" I repeat his question back to him, but somehow it's not the same.

"It has nothing to do with trust," Frank says. "You seem to forget, I could be arrested just for being with you, and then we'd never see each other again." He scowls and I'm afraid he's going to get in a bad mood, but instead he just changes the subject. "C'mon, now. Smile. And put your hands like this." Frank puts his hands on his hips and puckers up like Marilyn Monroe, and I do the same. We try other poses too, and I have to admit, it is kind of fun. And anyway, when the film is all used up, he puts the camera away and makes me feel so good, I forget about it.

When it's time to go, I change back into my regular clothes and head downstairs. I have my hand on the front doorknob, but then I hear Frank say, "Wait," and it makes me jump a little because I had no idea he was still in the house. I thought he was warming up the car.

I go into the kitchen, expecting to see Frank sitting on the counter, smoking a cigarette, but he's just standing there, staring out the window. I stand next to him, not too close and not too far away, and wait for him to say whatever he has to say.

"Vanessa," Frank finally says after a good five minutes, and for some reason I feel like screaming, *That's not my name, you idiot,* but of course I don't. I'm the one who's an idiot for telling him my name was Vanessa in the first place.

"Listen," Frank says, all serious. "I don't think we should see each other anymore."

Oh no. Not this again. Frank gets into these moods every once in a while, I don't know why. And I especially don't know why today, since we had such a great afternoon. He always comes around and changes his mind, though.

"Here." He reaches into his coat pocket and I think he's getting out the camera again, but then he puts something smaller on the counter. A little box. A little brown velvet jewelry box. For a split second I think he's giving me a present, but then I realize it's the box for Shirley's wedding ring and I get completely hysterical.

"Frank, what's the matter? What'd I do?" I keep my voice low and steady so I won't sound as scared as I feel.

"Vanessa." Frank gives this huge sigh, like my name, or what I told him is my name, is the reason for all the trouble in the world. "It's just that . . ." He looks right at me and his eyes are so sad and beautiful, I want to drown in them. "I don't know, babe. I just don't think I deserve you."

"Oh, Frank." What is he, nuts? God, he can be so weird sometimes. "If anything, Frank," I say, "*I* don't deserve *you*."

"Don't even say that, Vanessa. You deserve the best life has to offer, and don't you ever forget it."

"But Frank, *you're* the best life has to offer."

"You only think so, Vanessa." Frank looks down like a little boy who's done something naughty. "Vanessa," Frank says again, "I've been having some . . . some thoughts that I'm a little bit ashamed of."

I ignore the knot tightening in my belly. "What kind of thoughts, Frank?"

"Well," Frank looks at me again, and the poor guy seems like he's really in pain. "You're just so sexy and beautiful, I don't think I can stand it anymore."

Like that makes any sense. "Frank, what do you mean?"

"I mean, I can't hold out much longer, Vanessa. God, I dream about you all the time. But it isn't fair for me to pressure you into doing something you don't want to do or you're not ready to do. So I think it would be better if we just ended things." He looks over at Shirley's ring box and then he looks down again.

I can't even believe what I'm hearing. "You mean you want to go all the way?" See, it's like we're so connected, Frank can read my mind. This must be what they mean when they talk about finding your soul mate. You're two halves of the same whole. I'm so happy I almost laugh. "But Frank, that's what I want, too. I was going to tell you today. That's what I want for my birthday."

"You do?" Frank sounds totally surprised.

"Of course I do." What else would I want except to make him happy?

"When's your birthday?" Frank asks.

"Next Friday."

"C'mere, birthday girl." Frank opens his arms and gathers me into them. I lean back against him and let him hold me until he sighs like he's the happiest guy on the planet. Which I hope he is.

"Listen, Vanessa," Frank says, releasing me. "I don't want to see you until next Friday, you understand me?"

"But why, Frank?" My voice sounds shrill in my own ears, but I don't care. A whole week! We've never even gone more than a weekend without seeing each other, except for Thanksgiving, when I had Thursday and Friday off from school. "Frank, I don't want to go a whole week without seeing you."

"Don't whine, Vanessa."

"But why?"

"I said don't whine," Frank snaps. Then his voice softens. "I just want you to take some time and think this over so you're really sure about it."

"I *am* really sure."

"Vanessa, this is a very serious thing."

Duh, like I don't know that, Frank. What am I, a moron? I don't say anything so he goes on.

"I just want you to be sure—"

"I am sure."

"—that I'm the right guy," he says, ignoring me.

"Of course you're the right guy," I tell him. "Who else would be the right guy, Santa Claus?" I wait, but Frank doesn't laugh. "Of course you're the right guy, Frank," I say again. "God, before I met you I didn't know anything, I was just some stupid kid. But now, Frank, don't you get it?" I look at him, but he won't meet my eye. Still, I say it anyway: "Frank, I love you."

Silence. A long, loud, stupid, ugly silence. Frank doesn't do anything like say *I love you* back or take me in his arms and kiss me like I was hoping he would. He doesn't do or say anything, and the longer we stand there the more I feel like an idiot.

After a million years, Frank finally reaches for my hand and we just stand there with our fingers entwined not saying anything. Maybe hearing me say *I love you* got him too choked up to answer or something, because a lot of guys hate when a girl gets all emotional like that. But then Frank does say something, and it's the strangest thing, even for Frank. "I'll see you next Friday. And bring a raincoat. You hear me? Don't forget." And then he heads out the door and I follow.

TEN

This is horrible. The pits. Worse than the pits. Life without
Frank is one gigantic, stupid, worthless bore. It's like
when I'm with Frank I'm alive and when I'm not with
him I'm dead. It's only Saturday and I wouldn't be seeing
Frank today anyway, but still, knowing that I won't be
seeing him until next Friday is really getting me down.
And to top it all off, today I have to go to Donna Rizzo's
stupid sweet sixteen party.

A few months ago, Shirley actually asked me if *I*
wanted to have a sweet sixteen party. "Get real," I told
her. First of all, I'm not exactly sweet—sour sixteen is
more like it. And second of all, who would I invite? It's

not like I'm friends with any of the girls at my school. The only reason I got invited to Donna Rizzo's party is that her mother made her send an invitation to every single girl in our class.

If only I'd had a chance to intercept the mail before Shirley got her claws on it, she would never have known about it and I wouldn't have to go. But the mail comes in the morning while I'm still at school, so Shirley always gets to it first. And the day Donna's invitation came, Shirley met me at the door with this big smile on her face.

"What's this?" she asked, handing me an envelope with fancy lettering and a bright green frog sticker on it. She stood there breathing down my neck while I opened it, and then when she saw it was a bona fide invitation— in other words, her loser of a daughter actually had a social engagement—she got so excited I thought she was going to faint.

"Oh, Andrea, let me see." Shirley practically snatched the invitation out of my hand. "Ooh, it sounds like so much fun. What are you going to wear?"

"If you think it sounds so great, why don't you go?" I asked, but she just shot me a look that said *You are going to this party, young lady,* so here I am.

"Andrea, are you almost ready?" Shirley hollers up the stairs. Since Fred is at the office, she's my chauffeur today.

"Just a minute," I call down, even though I'm as ready as I'll ever be. I'm wearing my usual dungarees and black sweater, and I'm just stalling for time. But wouldn't you know it, Shirley decides to come upstairs and check out my attire.

"Andrea, you are not wearing that getup to a sweet sixteen party," she immediately says with a frown. "Don't you want to look nice for a change? Besides, Four Stars is a very fancy place. I'm sure they have a dress code."

"Well, then maybe I can't go," I say, my voice full of hope.

"Andrea, don't be silly. I'm sure there's something in here you can wear." And before I can stop her, Shirley yanks open my closet door and starts exploring.

"What about this?" Shirley pulls out a hanger and waves around the purple dress I wore to synagogue on Yom Kippur. My family is hardly religious, but we do go to temple on the High Holidays. Not that my parents pay attention to the service. Fred usually falls asleep with his hands clasped over his big belly, and Shirley gives herself whiplash from turning around every two seconds to see who just came in and what they're wearing.

"Shirley, I hate that dress."

"Why, what's wrong with it?" Shirley raises the hanger up to her neck, holds one sleeve out to the side, and lets the dress fall down her body, like she's checking to see how it would look on her. I guess the dress isn't so bad, as far as dresses go. It's got three-quarter sleeves and an empire waist, which made Shirley very happy when we bought it. In case you don't know, an empire waist is when the waistline of a dress is hitched up right below your boobs and it's supposed to make you look skinnier than you really are. I don't know why they call it that—maybe because it's supposed to make you look tall and thin like the Empire State Building.

"Andrea, I don't see anything else appropriate in here," Shirley says, once again inspecting my wardrobe. "You'll have to wear this. Too bad we're different sizes. Otherwise I could lend you something from my closet."

Thanks a lot, Shirley, I think, since that's a really mean thing to say. As if I don't know I'm twice as big as my own mother.

I put on the stupid dress and Shirley drives me to Four Stars for Donna's big birthday bash. God, I wish Ronnie were still here. We'd find a way to make this fun—maybe crash a wedding or bar mitzvah going on in another room, like I see out of the corner of my eye Cheryl Healy and Diane Carlson are doing. I'm sure they have no interest in going to a sweet sixteen, since the guest list won't include any boys.

I get rid of Shirley as fast as I can and go into the room where they're having Donna's party. As soon as I step inside, I see a table covered with a white tablecloth that has all these little cards set up with everyone's names and table numbers on them. I find my name and—just my luck—I'm at table thirteen. Not that I'm superstitious or anything, but still, this can't be a good sign. I make my way over to the table, which is all the way in the back, and sit down next to a bunch of girls I don't recognize. What do you know, Donna Rizzo has actually done me a favor by not seating me with anyone from our school.

"How do you know the bride?" the girl next to me asks in this totally sarcastic voice.

"The bride?"

"You know. The guest of honor. Miss Sweet Sixteen." She waves toward the front of the room where Donna is seated, surrounded by her friends.

"I go to her school," I say, getting the joke.

"We're her cousins from New Jersey," the girl says, gesturing to our tablemates. It takes me a minute but then I get it—of course I've been seated at the losers' table. Donna's cousins are the kind of girls no girl at my school would be caught dead talking to. Their hair is too high, their makeup too dark, their dresses too tight, their jewelry too gaudy.

Lunch is served, and since this is such a ritzy place, it's pretty fancy: stuffed mushrooms for the appetizer; a salad of lettuce, walnuts, pears, and crumbled blue cheese; and then an entrée of poached salmon, which freaks out one of the New Jersey cousins because, as she tells us, she almost choked to death on a salmon bone not too long ago. "So watch out for the bones," she says in this very serious tone, like they might sneak up behind us and murder us any second. Then we have cake and ice cream, and then Donna's mother announces it's time for the main event of the afternoon: watching Donna open all her gifts.

First, Horseface Hillary, who would do anything to be Donna's best friend, presents her with a memory cup that she's made for the occasion by putting sixteen pennies, a candle from Donna's cake, and a red plastic heart into a glass, filling it with water up to the brim, and then holding a lit candle upside down over it so that the wax from the candle drips onto the water and seals the whole thing shut forever. After everyone oohs and aahs over that, Marlene Pinkus, who's also dying to be in Donna's inner circle, starts bringing Donna's presents over to her table and volunteers to make Donna a hat out of all the ribbons and wrapping paper. Not to be outdone, Horseface says she'll write down who gave Donna what, so she won't mess up her thank-you notes. Once that's all settled, the show begins.

Donna's presents are no big surprise: makeup kits, jewelry, fuzzy sweaters, lots of records, and because of Donna's insane frog obsession, a million different frog items: frog pajamas, frog paperweights, frog music boxes, frog teapots, frog soap, frog pencils, frog pens, frog candles, at least twenty-five frog stuffed animals, a frog mobile, a frog umbrella. And last but not least, my gift: a book called *Frog and Toad Are Friends,* which I know is kind of babyish, but still, it's one of my favorite children's books about animals, and it does go with Donna's crazy obsession. Not that she seems to care.

After Donna finishes opening all her presents, Cheryl Healy stands up and Diane Carlson taps her fork against her glass to get everyone's attention. I guess the two of them got kicked out of whatever party they were crashing and decided to grace us with their presence after all.

"I'd like to read a poem in honor of the birthday girl," Cheryl says, her voice dripping with sweetness. Everyone sits up, impressed, but Cheryl doesn't fool me. She's definitely up to something.

"This is a found poem," Cheryl explains. "We learned

about them last week in English class. A found poem is a poem you find when you least expect it, like in a magazine or a catalog or during a conversation. So this is a poem I found right here at Donna's sweet sixteen party while she was opening her presents. It's called 'What Donna Will Say to Donald on Their Wedding Night.'"

And then, before anyone can stop her, Cheryl Healy reads off everyone's reactions to Donna's gifts:

"Ooh, look at that.
I've never seen anything like that before.
It's so cute. Can I feel it? Let me hold it.
It's so soft. Oh gross, it's kind of slippery.
Does it make noise if you squeeze it? Let me try.
This one is really unusual.
No, I've seen one like that before.
I've seen lots of those.
How does it work? Where's the instructions?
Do you have to wind it up? Put that part in here.
Wait, wait, don't be so impatient. It's stuck.
I think it's broken. It can't be broken already.
I can't get it out. It's totally stuck.
Let me try, I'm an expert.
Wow, I've wanted one of these my whole life.
It's so tiny, I always thought it would be bigger.
It's adorable.
Hey, smell this. This smells yummy. . . ."

"That's enough." Donna's mother stands up and glares at Cheryl Healy like she's going to kill her, but she doesn't want to cause a scene and ruin her darling daughter's party, which in my opinion is finally getting interesting.

"Thanks a lot, Cheryl Healy," Donna says, her face as pink as the dress Marlene Pinkus is wearing. "You've ruined my entire party!" Donna bursts into tears and Cheryl sits down with this huge grin on her face. I guess that'll teach Donna Rizzo to rat on her for smoking in the girls' room.

"Oh, lighten up, Cuz," one of my tablemates says. I look at her and she shrugs. "It's all just a comic opera," she says, gesturing around the room with one hand.

"It sure is," says Donna's other cousin.

And even though I don't know what that means exactly, I nod like I agree.

✖ ✖ ✖

Somehow I make it through the rest of the weekend okay, but on Monday, I feel totally miserable. The only reason I can usually take school at all is because I know I'm going to see Frank afterward. So Monday is really, really hard. When school is over I walk home, and then—I can't help it—I stop by the fence where Frank always picks me up and I wait, just in case.

I mean, you never know—maybe he changed his mind and decided he couldn't stand being apart from me for this long, like I can't stand being apart from him. But no, he doesn't show. I wait and wait even though it's freezing out and deep down inside I know he isn't coming, but still, it's not like I have anything better to do.

On Tuesday my heart hurts, you know, like I actually have this physical *pain* inside my chest like I'm having a heart attack or something even though I'm only fifteen. Wednesday is just as bad as Tuesday, and today, which is Thursday, I feel so depressed, I don't even bury my nose in a book at lunch like I usually do so no one will bother me. Big mistake on my part. Donald Caruso, who can always tell when I'm feeling particularly lousy, comes up to my table and immediately starts in.

"Isn't it a little *nippy* out today?" he asks, staring at my chest. I turn my back but of course he keeps at it. "Aw, what's the matter, Dee-Dee?" Donald says in this totally sarcastic voice, like he couldn't care less, which makes me want to scream *My name's not Dee-Dee, it's Vanessa, you idiot*. "What happened, huh?" Donald doesn't let up. "Oh, don't tell me, let me guess." He walks around until he's facing me, then scratches the side of his head like he's pretending to think, which is an activity he is clearly not capable of. "I know. You had a fight with your girlfriend, didn't you? What a *dee*-saster. Poor Dee-Dee."

"Oh, blow me," I say, like he's always saying to me.

"You want me to . . . That's *dee*-sgusting!" Donald starts making these gagging noises like he's going to puke. Then after a minute, he quits choking and chuckles. "It figures. Only a lezzie would say that."

"Takes one to know one." I shrug and then make myself busy with my ketchup and fries.

"Oh, go Suffolk yourself," Donald says, as if that's really clever, "since no one else will anyway."

"Oh yeah? Shows how much you know." The words just pop out of my mouth.

"Oh, you've got a boyfriend now?"

"Maybe I do and maybe I don't."

"Yeah, right." Donald rolls his eyes. "Like someone in this school would really find *you* attractive."

"Maybe he doesn't go to *this* school," I say, thinking Frank will kill me if I don't shut up.

"Well, what school does he go to?" Donald folds his arms.

"None of your beeswax." God, I feel like wiping the stupid smirk off his face with this packet of ketchup.

"Dee-Dee, the day you have a boyfriend will be the day I do blow you," Donald says, and then he sticks his tongue out and moves it all around his lips in this really slow, repulsive way. Then he laughs and takes off to sit at a table two rows in front of me, and every time I look up, he moves his tongue back and forth over his lips like he just ate something delicious, and I think I'm going to puke.

I get through the rest of the day, and on the way home, I actually start to feel better because I know to-morrow at this time, I'll be with Frank. I can hardly wait to see him and be with him and give myself to him. What a great birthday present.

God, I miss him so much right now, I could scream. I guess Frank was right to give me a whole week to think about things, you know, like how I feel about him and everything. The truth of the matter is, I'm totally nuts about the guy, I really am. You know what they say—absence makes the heart grow fonder, which I guess is true. I just like everything about him: the way he looks at me with those dark, dark eyes and the way he says "C'mere" in that sexy, sexy voice. Even his deformed pinkie is okay if I don't think about it too much. And when he touches me, whoa, that's the best. I can't even describe it. It's like my whole body's been sleeping for the past fifteen years and Frank just woke me up. Like he's the prince and I'm Sleeping Beauty, except asleep or awake, I'm not exactly beautiful.

I round the corner and see, much to my relief, that Shirley's car isn't in the driveway. So I let myself in and go straight up to Mike's room, which is where I'm getting the raincoat Frank asked me to bring. I wonder why he wants me to bring a raincoat of all things. Well, it's no weirder than some of the other things he's had me dress up in. He didn't say what kind of raincoat, so I hope Mike's is okay. Anyway, it's the best I can do.

I take it out of his closet and try it on. It's too big, of course, but I hope that won't matter. It looks more like a trench coat than a raincoat; Mike stole it from school one year, from the drama department when they were putting on *Guys and Dolls*. He said it made him look like a gangster, like it was the perfect coat to deal drugs in. It really is a pretty cool coat, kind of like what spies wear. I hope Frank likes it, not that it really matters. Knowing him, I probably won't keep it on very long.

The front door opens, which means Shirley's arrived upon the scene, so I take off Mike's raincoat, stuff it into my backpack, and head into my room before she can come upstairs and see what I'm up to. I guess now everything's in order for tomorrow's big event. I'm not really sure what to expect but I'm sure Frank will know what to do. And even though I'm not his first girl, I hope I'll be his last. I hope after tomorrow, he'll want to be with me and nobody else forever. That's what I'm going to wish for when I blow out the candles on my birthday cake. I'm sure Shirley will at least get me a cake, and birthday wishes have been known to come true. I mean, I didn't even wish for Frank, and he just showed up in my life like a miracle. So if that can happen, who knows what else life has in store?

ELEVEN

Happy birthday to me, happy birthday to me . . . I know it's pretty corny, but I do feel special today, even though it's just a day like any other day. December 17, 1971, my sixteenth birthday.

I get out of bed, shower and dress, and then pause at the top of the stairs because I hear someone in the kitchen, which is very unusual. Normally at this time Fred is stuck in traffic on the Long Island Expressway and Shirley is snoring away to beat the band. I stall as long as possible but I can't stay up here forever, so I finally go into the kitchen and there's Shirley in her green velour bathrobe and matching fuzzy slippers and there's Fred in his work clothes.

"Happy birthday," Fred and Shirley say in unison, like they rehearsed it.

Shirley's even set the table like she's Donna Reed or we're some other TV family from the fifties that actually eats breakfast together.

"Want a bagel?" she asks, which is totally bizarre because whenever Shirley makes me breakfast, which is pretty much never, she offers me Special K and skim milk, and if I'm lucky, half a grapefruit or a piece of plain dry toast. I guess everyone's on their best behavior today, so I don't say *Shirley you jest,* like I'm tempted to; I just say yes and sit down. But before I can take my first bite of bagel, Fred hands me an envelope.

"Thanks," I say, and when I tear it open, I almost have a heart attack because there, taped to the pink, flowery card that says *Happy Sweet Sixteen to Our Darling Daughter,* is something I never thought I'd see in my entire life: a car key.

"What's this?" I ask Fred, since I know better than to think the Rents are giving me wheels for my birthday. Mike doesn't even own a car yet, and he'd totally blow his stack if his baby sister got one first.

"It's a key to my car for when you get your learner's permit," Fred says, and then he attacks his fried eggs, which are totally runny and disgusting so I try not to look. "I'm going to teach you how to drive, just like I taught Mike."

Oh great. This is not something to look forward to, because if I remember correctly, there was a lot of screaming and door-slamming and stormy silences at the dinner table between the time Mike got his learner's permit and the time he got his driver's license.

"Thanks a lot, Fred," I say, pocketing the key. I figure we can discuss the driving lessons another time.

"And here's another present," Shirley says, handing me a little box all wrapped up in silver paper and tied with a shiny white bow. Usually we wait and do presents at night, but I guess sixteen is more special than regular birthdays.

I take off the wrapping paper and almost gasp because the box is exactly the same as the one Shirley keeps her wedding ring in. Same size, same shape, same color, same everything. Shirley's never said anything about the ring so I'm pretty sure she hasn't noticed it's missing, but still, this box makes me nervous. The lid even creaks exactly like Shirley's wedding ring box, which freaks me out even more, but I just make myself act normal, whatever that means, and peek inside.

It's a locket. A gold locket shaped like a heart with tiny flowers etched into it. I have to admit it's really pretty, even though it's not exactly my style. I'm not the kind of girl that goes in for hearts and flowers, which Shirley would realize if she ever bothered to open her eyes. But for some reason, I don't want to hurt her feelings today, so I don't say anything. It's weird, but like everyone else, I'm on my best behavior, too.

"Here, I'll put it on for you." Shirley takes the locket out of my hands before I can say anything and steps behind me. I lift all my hair off my neck so she can fasten the chain.

"It looks beautiful," Shirley says when I turn around. "My mother got it from her mother when she was sixteen and she gave it to me when I was sixteen. I've been saving it for you ever since you were a little girl."

"Thanks, Shirley."

"You're welcome." She tilts her head a little to the left, the same way Ronnie's toy poodle does when you say to her, "Pompom, want to go out?" I know that's my cue to give Shirley a kiss on the cheek, so I do. And then before I can step back, Shirley grabs me with both arms and gives me this enormous, bone-crushing hug, which is something she's never done before. And believe me, for someone as skinny as a cigarette, Shirley's a lot stronger than she looks. I put my arms around her and hug her back because I don't know what else to do, and I'm surprised at how fragile she feels. Like I could snap her bones in half if I wanted to.

Finally Shirley releases me and steps back. "Do you really like it?" she asks, reaching out to adjust the locket.

"Yeah, Shirley," I say, and I mean it too. It's pretty cool to think that Shirley had this present waiting for me even before I was born. Though I wonder if Shirley was really saving it for Melissa, my sister who died. Since she was older, she would have turned sixteen first. Maybe we would have shared it. Or fought over it. Except that if she didn't die, I wouldn't even be here, so I guess that's all beside the point.

I eat my toasted bagel and then hurry off to school. And who's the first person I see when I get there?

Donald Caruso, of course.

"Ooh, Dee-Dee," he says the minute I take off my coat. "Your girlfriend sent you a locket. You must be *dee*-lirious with joy."

"Listen, you moron." I go right up in his face. "This is a family heirloom and it's the only thing I have from my great-grandmother who died in the Holocaust, so just lay off, you hear me?"

"Sorry." Donald actually looks apologetic as he backs away. Of course, what I said wasn't true, but I'm especially not in the mood for Donald today. I'm not in the mood for anything except that final bell, which is taking forever to ring. I keep looking at the clock and this is how I tell time: four hours and twenty minutes till Frank, three hours and fifteen minutes till Frank, two hours till Frank, one hour till Frank . . .

Finally school is over, thank God. I don't think I could sit still one minute longer. I grab my knapsack and peek inside to make sure Mike's raincoat is still in there, which is silly, since it can't exactly open my locker and walk away. Then I head out the door without even buttoning up my jacket and it's not exactly July. But I don't care. I get to the spot where I usually meet Frank a little early, hoping that he'll be there already because he just can't wait to see me, the way I can't wait to see him. But he's not here yet, which doesn't really surprise me. Frank isn't one to mess with our routine.

I stamp my feet a little, trying to stay warm while I wait for him. It's so cold out, I wish I was in Bessie's barn with her, but I'm sure I won't be out here much longer. Frank will be here any minute. While I wait for him, I look at my new locket. I open it and shut it, and then for some reason, I decide to take it off and put it in my pocket next to my lucky shell, because what if Frank sees it and thinks some guy gave it to me instead of Shirley? Then he'll get all mad and jealous. Yeah, like what guy would ever give me a locket, Batman?

So where is Frank already? I don't have a watch on, but I know it's past the time when he usually gets here. I can't even think about the possibility that he's not going to show up, so I start walking up and down a little, waving my arms to keep the blood flowing, and then, just because I feel like it, I break into this ridiculous cheer: "Frank, Frank he's our man, if he can't do it, no one can!" And I shake my hands out in front of my chest like I'm holding two pompoms or something. And then, just as I start in with, "Two, four, six, eight, Frankie Boy is really great," I hear his car take the corner and my heart starts beating so fast I'm afraid it's going to explode right there in my chest.

"How come you're late?" I ask as soon as I get in the car. God, what a moron I am. I sound just like Shirley when Fred gets home late from the office. Shirley says I never think before I speak and for once in her life she's right.

But Frank doesn't get mad, which is a nice surprise; you never know with Frank. "I just wanted to give you one last chance to change your mind," he says, putting his hand on my knee as he starts to drive. "This is a very serious thing, Vanessa."

Duh, like I don't know that. I mean, you could get a horrible disease like syphilis and die from what we're about to do, or you could get pregnant and have a baby if you're not careful. Which is weird when you think about it. Sex really is a matter of life and death.

"I didn't change my mind" is all I say, since I don't want to get all intense and heavy on Frank. Then I sit back in my seat and stare at his hand. It's so good to see it again—weird pinkie and all—I feel like, I don't know, picking it up and squeezing it or kissing it even. I also feel like peeking into the backseat to see if Frank got me a birthday present, but I don't dare turn around.

Frank doesn't say one word the rest of the way to the house and I'm worried he forgot it's my birthday, but now isn't exactly the time to remind him. I mean, he did show up and everything, didn't he? Yeah, but he hasn't even wished me a happy birthday. It wouldn't kill him to at least say that. I'm kind of mad, but when we get to the house I see what a big fat idiot I am because Frank has decorated the entire downstairs of the house with streamers and balloons and everything. There's a banner that says *Sweet Sixteen* hung up in the kitchen too, and on the counter there's even a little cake with pink and white frosting and sixteen candles in it.

"Frank, you're the best," I say, giving him a hug, and even though he's not usually into big displays of affection, he holds me close and strokes my hair for a minute. Then he gets out his matches and lights all the candles and while I think of a wish, he lights himself a butt. I don't know what to wish for since I already have Frank, which is everything I want. I think a minute more and then wish that this year would fly by so I'll turn seventeen and then Frank and I won't have to sneak around anymore and we can be together forever. Then I take a deep breath and blow out all my candles on the first try, which means my wish will definitely come true.

I take the candles out of my cake, cut two pieces with my Swiss army knife, and serve them to us on plates that say *Sweet Sixteen*. Frank only takes one little bite of his, and you'd think I'd be too nervous to eat too, but I actually finish my piece and have another.

When I'm done eating, Frank says, "Let's go upstairs," so we do. I thought maybe he'd tell me to go upstairs first and put on the raincoat, but it's weird, he made such a big deal out of me bringing it, but he hasn't even mentioned it yet. I take my knapsack upstairs anyway and follow Frank into the room where the sleeping bags are.

"Get undressed," Frank says, unzipping his jacket.

I drop my knapsack in the corner. "Don't you want me to put on an outfit or something?"

"Yeah, your birthday suit, birthday girl," he says, and then he chuckles at his joke, which is so funny I forgot to laugh.

"Can't I put an outfit on?" I ask Frank, and even though he's annoyed, he says okay. I don't know why, but I feel a little scared to be totally naked if he's going to be totally naked too. I change into my black lace outfit, come back into the sleeping bag room, and then for the first time ever, watch Frank take off his clothes.

First he bends over to take off his work boots and

socks, but as soon as his bare feet hit the floor, he puts his socks right back on. "Criminy, it's cold in here," he says, like that's news to me. It's been freezing for the past month, but how would Frank know that? He's never even taken off his jacket.

Next he unbuckles his belt and drops it on the floor, where it curls up like a sleeping snake. Then he undoes his pants and lets them drop to his ankles and I don't mean to stare, but Frank has the hairiest legs I've ever seen. He's wearing white boxer shorts and he leaves them on while he takes off his shirt and his undershirt, and I try to keep my face still so I don't look shocked because Frank is just one big fat hairball, he really is. I mean, Fred has some hair on his chest and so does Mike, but Frank— I hate to say this—he's like a total ape. He's got thick dark hair on his chest, his stomach, his arms, and even his shoulders, too.

Frank drops his clothes on the floor and then just stands there in his underwear. "Don't be scared, Vanessa," he says, so I guess he can tell I am. "C'mere, baby." He speaks in his nice, soothing voice, which makes me happy. I go to him and let him hug me a little. Then he releases me and speaks gruffly. "Get the rain-coat."

I bend over for my knapsack and pull out Mike's trench coat. It's pretty wrinkled from being balled up all day, but I don't think Frank will notice. I shake the coat out and hold it up. "Do you want me to put it on?"

Frank startles and looks taken aback for a minute. He stares at the coat and then at me. His eyes go back and forth—the coat, my face, the coat, my face—and then this look comes over him that I've never seen before. He seems puzzled or confused, but he's kind of sad too, or maybe even a little scared, and then he starts to laugh. And I mean really laugh, not his usual snort or chuckle or smirk. Frank is completely hysterical. We're talking hyena here. He actually has to hold on to the wall for support, and his whole body shakes as he laughs, roars, guffaws; he even doubles over and slaps his knee. I don't even have a clue here and I wish somebody would please tell me what in the world is so funny. I feel like a complete imbecile standing around almost naked holding Mike's wrinkled raincoat while Frank gets his jollies. And I'm mad, too, because this is not the way I thought my birthday would be.

Frank straightens up, looks at me, smiles, and then— I can tell he doesn't want to, but he just can't help himself—he loses it again. "Oh, Vanessa, you poor baby." Frank finally gets it together and drops down to his knees on top of the sleeping bags. "C'mere, birthday girl." He holds out his hand and I take it, even though I don't really want to, and let him pull me down on the floor.

"A raincoat"—he smiles and I'm afraid he's going to lose it again but he doesn't—"a raincoat is slang for a condom."

Oh my God, I don't believe it. He meant a condom? I feel like such a moron holding Mike's raincoat, I want to just rip it to shreds, or ball it up and chuck it out the window. I am just so unbelievably stupid.

"Frank," I say, trying to control my voice so I don't cry. "Why didn't you just say condom if you meant condom?"

"Vanessa, I thought you'd know what I meant," he says. "Why in the world would I want you to bring a raincoat?"

Because you're weird, Frank, I want to say but of course I don't.

"When I was your age, we always called them raincoats," Frank goes on, and I feel like asking, *When was that, Frank, 1922?* "You know, raincoats, rubbers, anything that keeps you dry."

I can hardly even look at him, I feel so dumb. "I'm sorry, Frank," I mumble into his chest. I wouldn't even blame him for getting mad, but he doesn't.

"Oh, Vanessa." He lays me down and takes me in his arms, the way he knows I like. "You really are sixteen, aren't you?"

No, Frank, I think, *I'm a hundred and twelve,* but I can't stay mad for long, especially when he holds me so soft and so tight.

"Are we still going to do it?" I ask after a while.

"Oh, baby, I want to, you know how much I want to. But we can't." Frank's voice is sad, and I feel like crying again, I'm such a total failure.

"But it's my birthday and I wanted it to be special," I say, and then I can't help it, I do begin to blubber. "Can't we do it anyway? I won't get pregnant, I promise. And even if I do, I'll take care of it."

Frank stops stroking me and sits up sharply, making

me sit up too. "Now you listen to me, Vanessa," he says, and he's not mad exactly, just stern. "Don't you ever *ever* think of not using protection, you hear me? You've always got to look out for yourself. I don't care what kind of line a guy gives you. Guys can't be trusted. Believe me, I'm a guy. I know."

Frank's eyes are blazing, like he's really mad at someone, but I don't think it's me. And what is he now, my father? What's with the lecture?

"Frank, what are you talking about? What guy? I don't want to ever be with anyone but you," I say, hoping he'll say, *I don't want to ever be with anyone but you either,* but of course he doesn't. He just shushes me and tells me to lie down.

"Shut your eyes now and I'll give you your birthday present," he says and then he finally does what I've wanted him to do since the day I met him: he kisses me. A nice soft, sweet, wet, juicy kiss that practically takes my breath away. I don't even mind the cigarette taste so much because Frank's mouth is just heaven.

"Did you like that?" Frank asks, and before I can even answer, he says we need to get going and pulls away from me. I turn my back and change into my regular clothes and put Mike's raincoat back in my knapsack. We leave the house kind of messy—there's nothing to even cover the cake with—but Frank doesn't care, so why should I? All I care about is whether I'll see him on Monday or not but of course I'm too afraid to pop the question. But Frank reads my mind as usual because the minute we're back in the car he says, "Do you think you can bring a raincoat on Monday, Vanessa?" And he slows down his voice and raises his eyebrows when he says the word *raincoat* just to make sure I know what he means.

"Can't you bring it?" I ask as he puts the screwdriver into the ignition. The VW starts up right away, so maybe his friend Lloyd finally fixed it.

"Vanessa, it's always the woman's responsibility to take care of that," Frank says in his stern voice.

"Okay," I say, even though that isn't fair. But if you really think about it, I guess fair or not fair, it's true, because I'm the one who could get pregnant, not Frank. And anyway, I have other things to worry about besides what's fair and what isn't. Like where in the world am I supposed to get a condom? Luckily I have all weekend to figure that out.

TWELVE

After Frank drops me off and waves, I wave back and start walking home fast, not because I'm in a rush to get there but because it's pretty chilly out. While I walk, I think about Frank, of course. It's funny; you'd think I'd be all happy to see him today—and I was, don't get me wrong, but part of me felt mad, too. I guess I'm not really mad at him so much, I'm mad at the situation—you know, how we have to sneak around and stuff. If Frank and I were allowed to have a normal relationship, he could take me out to dinner or something (yeah, right, like Fred would ever let him). As it is, we have to keep our relationship a secret for another whole year, which is really, really hard.

I pick up the pace because it's getting colder by the minute and some snowflakes are even coming down. And then, as soon as I turn our corner, I see something that almost gives me a full-fledged heart attack: in addition to Shirley's car beached in its usual spot in our driveway, Fred's car is parked out on the street. I don't ever remember Fred coming home this early. Something must be wrong, really wrong, like World War III broke out when I wasn't looking, which is exactly what would happen if Fred ever found out about me and Frank.

I drag myself up the driveway and reach into my pocket for my keys but before I can even fish them out, the door opens.

"Surprise!"

"Mike, wow!" I can't believe it: Mike flew home for my birthday. I'm so happy to see him I start to cry a little, like that makes sense. He gives me a huge, squashy hug, and then I hang up my coat and go into the kitchen, where Shirley is, of all things, cooking. And I don't mean just warming up a TV dinner in the toaster oven either. She's actually standing at the stove, wearing an apron, with a spatula in her hand. And Fred is sitting at the table, reading the *New York Times*. This is so weird, it's like I'm on a movie set and everyone knows exactly how to play their part except me.

"I can't believe you're sixteen," Mike says, coming up behind me. "Hey, you get your learner's permit yet?"

"Mike, I was in school all day, remember?" I shoot him a look. "I didn't have time to visit the Department of Motor Vehicles."

"We can go Monday after school if you want," Shirley says, opening the refrigerator and taking out some butter. Oh great. Why is she being so buddy-buddy all of a sudden? What am I supposed to tell her? *Sorry, Shirley, I have an appointment to lose my virginity Monday at three o'clock. Maybe Tuesday.* Yeah, right.

"Let's go for a ride right now," Mike says.

"She can't drive without a permit," Fred's disembodied voice reminds us from behind the newspaper, like I'm just dying to get behind the wheel, which I'm not. What if I have an accident, even one that isn't my fault, like what happened to my family that time in the Catskills when my sister was killed?

"Supper will be ready in forty-five minutes," Shirley says, like Mike and I care.

"Don't worry, we'll be back." Mike grabs Fred's keys, which are sprawled across the kitchen table. "C'mon, Squirt, let's make like a tree and leave."

"One second." I dash down the hallway to use the bathroom and make sure I look all right. It's not like Mike will be able to tell I've just been with Frank or anything, but still I wash my face, rinse my mouth, and comb my hair just to be sure.

"Ready, Squirt?" Mike asks, and when I nod, he says, "Exit stage left," and sidesteps out the door.

"See you soon," I call out to Fred and Shirley as I follow Mike out to the car. "You look good," I tell Mike. "I can't believe how long your hair is."

"Neither can Fred," Mike says, unlocking the car. "You want to drive or ride shotgun?"

"Mike, you know I can't drive yet."

Mike shrugs. "Suit yourself," he says, and then gets into the car.

I slide into the passenger seat and buckle up while Mike starts the engine. "So, where are we going?" I ask as he backs out of the driveway.

"Nowhere fast," Mike says, which I guess is supposed to be funny, but it isn't because it's true. "So, how are you?"

"Fine, how are you?"

"Fine, how are you?"

"Fine, how are you?"

"Cut!" Mike slices the air with his right hand, like he's a movie director stuck with a stupid actress who can't do anything right. "How's life with the Rents?"

"Awful."

"Really? What a surprise." Mike turns right and starts driving through our development. "What's Shirley up to these days?"

"What do you think?" I ask Mike, who doesn't bother to answer. "She's either out shopping or having lunch with her friends or home smoking her cigarettes and watching stupid TV."

"What a life." Mike makes a left turn and shakes his head. "How about King Frederick the First?" he asks. "Still spending every waking hour at the office?"

"And then some," I say. "How can he stand to stare into people's disgusting mouths all day long? Gross."

"If that's what he's really doing."

"What do you mean?" I look over at Mike.

"I don't know, Squirt. Don't you ever wonder if Fred's getting a little action on the side?"

"What kind of action?"

"What kind of action?" Mike steals a glance at me. "Squirt, use your im-ag-i-na-tion." His voice goes up at the end of the word.

I stare at my brother, who can only be talking about one thing. "Do you really think so?"

Mike shrugs. "Beats me. How should I know? It's just a thought." Mike pauses and then says almost to himself, "You couldn't blame the poor guy, though. His wife certainly hasn't put out in years."

"So? Maybe she doesn't feel like putting out," I say, mad all of a sudden. "And anyway, they're married, Mike. So even if Shirley doesn't want to do it, that doesn't give Fred an excuse to go do it with someone else."

Mike looks at me like I've sprouted an extra head all of a sudden. "Wow, Squirt. I've never heard you take Shirley's side on anything before."

I'm a little surprised myself, so I don't say anything more and Mike keeps driving. We pass our old elementary school, a park, and the public library.

"Anyway, like you said, it's just a thought," I say, staring out the window. "And here's another thought: Shirley's hardly ever home either. Maybe *she's* getting a little action on the side."

Mike laughs, which makes me mad again.

"What?" I say. "Lots of people lead double lives, you know."

"Oh yeah? Like who?"

Me, I almost say, but I can't get the word out. "I don't know. Like spies."

Mike raises one eyebrow at me. "You think Shirley's a spy?"

"No." I scowl at him. "But maybe she's not out with her friends all day. Maybe that's an excuse. Maybe she's meeting someone on the sly. Maybe she's . . . Maybe she's . . ." I struggle to imagine our mother spending her time with a tall, dark, handsome stranger in some exciting locale, but it's impossible.

"The Secret Life of Shirley Kaplan." Mike outlines the words with one hand like they're spelled out on the marquee of a movie theater. "I don't think so, Squirt. Anyway, enough about them; let's talk about us. Now, you didn't hear this from me, but"—he pauses for dramatic effect—"I'm dropping out again."

"Mi-ike!" I'm only halfway listening because I'm still thinking about Fred and Shirley and the possibilities of their secret lives, but when Mike says this, I snap to full attention. "Mike, Fred is going to totally kill you."

"I know. Maybe I should just end it all right now." He jerks the car to the right and heads straight for a telephone pole.

"Mike, what are you, crazy?" I lunge for the wheel, but he elbows me out of the way and steers us back onto the road. "Relax, Squirt. Sheesh, what, have you lost your sense of *yuma*?" he asks in a fake Brooklyn accent.

"So, like, what are you going to do?"

"Get on the expressway," he says, which is really dumb, since it's rush hour.

"No, Mike, really."

He doesn't answer until he's driven out of our development, turned up the entry ramp and merged us into the traffic. "For your information, I'm going to finish out the semester just in case I ever decide to go back, which is highly, highly"—he puts his thumb and first finger up to his lips and sucks air in like he's smoking a joint— ". . . unlikely. I have two finals this week, which I'll take even though I'll probably flunk them."

"Mike, can't you study even a little?"

"What's the point, Squirt?" He waits for an answer, but we both know I don't have one.

"So then, once I'm done with my tests," Mike goes on, "the Parental Eunuchs think I'm coming home, but— and keep this under your hat, Squirt—your big bro is going to Hawaii."

"Hawaii?" I'm so surprised, he might as well have said Jupiter. "What are you going to do in Hawaii?"

"Pick avocados."

"Mike, be serious."

"I am serious."

"What do you know about picking avocados?"

"Nothing I can't learn."

"And how are you going to get money to go to Hawaii?"

"It's not going to cost that much. I'm going to hitchhike to San Francisco and then hop a plane from there."

"Hitchhike? Mike, isn't that kind of dangerous?"

Mike shakes his head like he can't believe what he's hearing. "Squirt, haven't you ever read *On the Road*?"

"Nope."

"Well, you should. It's by Jack Kerouac, one of the coolest guys ever. He was friends with Allen Ginsberg, who wrote 'Howl,' that poem I told you about, remember?"

"Yeah, so, what's this got to do with anything?"

"The point is, I'm not college material, we both know that. I want to see the country, man. Meet new people, have some adventures."

"Well, you're still going to need money," I tell him, folding my arms.

"Not a problem, Squirt. I've sold a few things lately—"

"Mike, don't tell me you're dealing again."

"Shhh." Mike holds one finger up to his lips and looks quickly around the car like he's totally paranoid. "For all we know, Big Daddy's bugged the Caddie."

"Just do me a favor and don't get caught," I say, staring out the window. I can't believe Mike's going to Hawaii. That's like ten thousand miles away.

"Don't worry about me, Squirt." Mike pulls into a rest area and shuts off the car, but still I won't look at him. "Hey, c'mon, no need to worry. I have the perfect cover."

"What?" I finally turn around.

"Look out there, Squirt. What do you see?"

"Cars, trees, clouds . . ."

"And litter, right?" Mike gestures toward a black plastic bag crumpled up near the side of the highway. "What I do, see, is take my dope stash and put it in an empty Coke can. Then I put the Coke can next to me on the ground, like someone threw it there. When I get a ride, I grab the can and off I go. If a cop picks me up for hitching, I leave it there and I'm clean. True, I forfeit the dope, but that can't be helped. Brilliant, isn't it?"

I have to admit it's a pretty good plan, but I don't want to encourage Mike so I pretend I'm thinking it over.

"Oh, don't be mad, Squirt. It's your birthday, for cryin' out loud. And speaking of . . ." Mike digs into his pockets. "How about starting the celebration a little early?"

I don't even have to turn around to know he's holding a joint. "Mike, you're going to smell up Fred's car, you moron."

"Takes one to know one," Mike says, opening his door.

"Hey, shut that, it's freezing out."

"Chicken," Mike says, getting out of the car. I glare at him through the windshield but then I bundle up and get out too.

"Walk this way," Mike says, and he starts walking all bent over with his arms swinging like an ape. I laugh and start walking like a monkey too.

"So tell me, Andrea Robin, what's new like this?" Mike asks in a perfect imitation of our grandmother. He lights the joint and inhales as we stroll around the parking lot, which is completely empty except for Fred's car and one big truck parked way down at the other end.

"Nothing," I say, but of course he knows better.

"Nothing, my ass."

"Your ass is grass."

"No, this is grass," he says, holding the joint out to me. "C'mon, try it, Squirt. It won't kill you. Who knows, you might even like it."

"I doubt it. You know how much I hate smoke."

"How can you know you hate it if you've never even tried it?" Mike takes another toke. "Please, *mameleh*, do it for me," he says like he's our grandmother again.

"Oh, all right." I take the joint. "What do I do?"

"Inhale and hold the smoke in for as long as possible." He takes the joint back to demonstrate. Then I grab it and do what he does, but of course it only takes half a second for me to start coughing my brains out.

"Now, as I was saying"—Mike pats me on the back—"you can fool Fred and Shirley some of the time, and Shirley and Fred all of the time, but you can't fool your big brother Mike anytime. So where were you after school? And don't give *me* any BS about being at the library."

"Well, if you must know," I say, looking down at the ground, "I happen to have a boyfriend." I'm embarrassed and proud to tell him.

"A *what*?" Mike sputters like he's about to swallow the joint.

"A boyfriend," I repeat, pronouncing the word slowly, like he's suddenly lost command of the English language. "Hello, I *am* a girl, remember? Oh, give me that." I reach for the joint and inhale again, just for the heck of it. This time I don't cough.

"So who's the unlucky"—I glare at Mike and he corrects himself—"I mean the lucky guy? Is he in your class?"

"Nope." Mike waits for me to offer up more information. "He's older."

"What, a junior?"

"Nope."

"He's a senior?" Mike's eyebrows shoot up.

"Nope."

"What the heck is he then, a college guy?"

"Well, if you must know, he's not in school."

"He works?"

"I guess so."

"What do you mean, you guess so?"

"Hey, c'mon, Mike. I didn't give him the third degree."

Mike takes a toke while he thinks this over. "So where did you meet this guy?"

"Around."

"Around, huh?" Mike thinks this over too, while he digs a roach clip out of his pocket. It looks like a bloodshot eyeball with something like a paper clip on the end. "Here." He holds the roach to my lips so I can take a final hit. I don't really like it so much and I don't see what the big deal is. I mean, I feel perfectly normal, which is pretty funny when you think about it. Like I could ever be normal, let alone perfect.

Mike takes one more toke and then puts out the roach and pockets it. "Does this guy have a name?"

"Frank." It's the first time I've ever said his name out loud to anyone.

"Frank what?"

"Frankfurter."

"Frankfurter?"

"No, Frankenstein," I say, and then I crack up like I

just said the funniest thing in the world. I laugh and laugh until I give myself a stomachache, and even then I can't stop.

"Is somebody stoned?" Mike asks, but I can't answer because I'm still totally hysterical. Finally after a million years, I calm down and catch my breath. "Here, have some of these." Mike takes two small bags of M&M's out of his jacket pocket. "Do you want the plain ones or the peanuts?"

"The peanuts," I say, only it sounds like I said *the penis,* which makes me hysterical again.

"Hey, Squirt, think fast," Mike says, and then he spins around on his heel and tosses a bag of candy at me. I'm still laughing too hard to catch it, but it doesn't matter. Mike just shakes his head and pours half a bag of plain M&M's down his throat while I pull myself together. When I finally do, I pick up my bag of M&M's, open it, and toss one into my mouth. It tastes fantastic. First I suck off the candy shell part, then I let the chocolate part melt all over my tongue, and finally I bite into the peanut. Wow. I don't ever remember M&M's tasting this good before. I eat them slowly, one at a time, as we head back to the car, first the red ones, then the yellows, then the browns, and last of all the greens.

"So this guy Frank," Mike says when we get back to the car.

"Yeah?"

"He treats you okay?"

"Yeah, sure."

"What do you guys do?"

"What do you mean, what do we do?"

"I mean, does he take you to the movies, does he take you bowling . . . ?"

I've never been able to lie to Mike. "No, he doesn't really take me places."

"What do you mean, he doesn't take you places? What do you do when you're together?"

"God, what do you think, Mike? He's a guy, I'm a girl. What do you think we do when we're together? Play poker? Use your im-ag-i-na-tion." I throw his own words back at him.

"Blah blah blah blah blah blah." Mike covers his ears and shuts his eyes like a little kid who wants to block out what a grown-up is saying.

"Mike!"

He opens his eyes and takes his hands away from his ears.

"That's better."

"Listen, Squirt. Let me just ask you one thing." Mike narrows his eyes at me. "Frank isn't, like, pressuring you, if you catch my drift?"

"No." I'm, like, pressuring him, in fact, but of course I don't say that to Mike.

"I don't know." Mike still isn't satisfied. "You're kind of young to be going out with an older guy."

"Mike, I'm sixteen."

"Duh. Why do you think I came home, birthday girl?" When Mike calls me that, I remember Frank saying it and I shudder a little. "You cold?" Mike pitches his M&M's bag and unlocks the driver's side of the car.

"Mike!" He knows I hate it when he litters. I go after the trash and try to stuff it in my pocket, but my hand hits something. "Hey, look what Shirley gave me." I show him the locket and make him hold up all my hair so I can fasten the chain around the back of my neck. "And remember this?" I take my shell out of my pocket and hold it up too.

"No, what's that?"

"My lucky shell. You gave it to me, don't you remember? Like six years ago when you cut school and went to Jones Beach."

"When *I* cut school?" Mike asks, like he's the kind of guy who would never even think about doing such a thing. "*I* never cut school, Squirt. You must be thinking about your other big brother."

"C'mon, Mike. Don't you even remember giving this to me?" I hold my shell up to his face but he just shrugs and shakes his head. Then he gets in the car and I go around to my side, but I feel totally sad all of a sudden, and I'm afraid if I look at him, I'll cry. So I get in and just look at my shell instead. It's not even a whole shell, really; it's just a piece of one, and it's an ugly, stupid pink too. Suddenly I'm completely disgusted with it and I open the car window and throw it into the traffic.

"Squirt, did you just litter?" Mike turns to look at me. "Don't you know you can get fined fifty bucks for that?"

I don't answer him and after a while he turns on the radio and switches stations until Bob Dylan's twangy nasal voice fills the air. Mike loves Bob Dylan, but if you want my opinion, the guy can't sing to save his life. I think Mike likes him because he gives him hope: if one Jewish guy who can't carry a tune can get rich and famous, then why not another?

"This is a really cool song, Squirt," Mike says, starting to sing along. "Listen to the words. It's pure poetry."

"How's your poetry?" I ask, but he puts his finger up to his lips, telling me to be quiet so he can concentrate on the song.

"Um, Mike, I hate to interrupt you, but . . ."

"Quiet, Squirt, this is the best part."

"But Mike, we missed our exit."

"What?" Mike comes to and looks around. "Oh well," he says with a grin. "Welcome to Pennsylvania."

"Yeah," I say, shaking my head. Mike's way of saying "oops" is "Welcome to Pennsylvania" because two years ago when he and some friends tried to go to Woodstock for the biggest rock-and-roll concert of all time, they were so stoned they got completely lost, which they didn't even realize until they passed a sign that said WELCOME TO PENNSYLVANIA. When they finally got themselves turned around and heading back to upstate New York, they got stuck in this huge traffic jam and missed the whole concert. And that, ladies and gentleman, is basically the story of my big brother's life.

We get off at the next exit, get back on going in the right direction, and finally pull into the driveway half an hour late for dinner. But still, Mike's not in a big rush to get out of the car.

"Here," he says, handing me a little bottle.

"What's this?"

"Visine. For your eyes, so they won't look so red." I use it; then he takes the bottle out of my hand, tilts his head back, and puts some drops in his eyes. "And take a piece of gum too."

"Mike, we should really go in," I say, popping a piece of Wrigley's Spearmint into my mouth.

"Not so fast," he says, resting his head back against the seat. "Listen, Squirt. Have the Rental Units met this guy Frank yet?"

I stare at him. "Get real."

"Maybe they should."

"Yeah, well, maybe they should buy you a ticket to Honolulu."

"Squirt." Mike picks his head up and frowns. "Listen, maybe I should meet him while I'm home."

"How long are you staying?" I try to keep my voice calm.

"Just until Sunday. I told you I have tests next week, I have to fly back."

"Well, Frank's away for the weekend," I say, which is sort of true. I mean, he's away somewhere, I just don't know where.

"What kind of guy goes away for the weekend when it's his girlfriend's birthday?" Mike asks. "You sure this guy is on the level?"

"I'm sure," I say in a voice I hope is convincing.

"I don't know, I just don't like it." Mike shakes his head. "How come if this guy is so great you've never told me about him before?"

"Mike, you know Fred is always listening on the upstairs extension," I say, my voice full of exasperation. "Listen, Frank's a great guy. Really, he is."

"Well, just be careful, okay, Andi? You can't really trust guys. I'm a guy—believe me, I know." I swear, I get goose bumps when he says that, I really do. That is just too weird, for Frank and Mike to say the exact same thing to me on the exact same day. "So, is he going to take you out or something when he gets back or what?"

"Don't worry, Mike, we're definitely going to have a celebration." Boy, are we ever.

"You just make sure he treats you good, or else." Mike reaches for the door handle.

"Or else what? You'll fly back from Hawaii and cream him?"

"You better believe it. C'mon." And the two of us get out of the car and go into the house for my big birthday supper.

THIRTEEN

As soon as Mike and I walk in, Shirley announces that
dinner is ready, so we head into the kitchen. Shirley
serves London broil to Fred and Mike and gives me a veg-
etable and cheese omelette which is actually almost edi-
ble. Then she piles some chicken slices with the skin cut
off on top of the little postage scale she keeps on the
counter to measure out her Weight Watchers–approved
portions. By the time she brings her plate over to the
table, Fred is holding his empty dish up in the air, which
means he's ready for seconds, so she has to serve him
again before she gets to sit down.

Nobody really says much at dinner, I don't know

why. Maybe because we're not used to eating together as a family anymore. Or maybe since we're all on our best behavior for my birthday, no one wants to bring up anything that could start a fight. Which basically rules out everything.

When we're done eating, Fred clears his throat. "Why don't you and Mike retire to the living room?" he asks.

You mean Shirley's actually going to clean up? I raise my eyebrows in surprise and then quickly vacate the premises with Mike. And then just as I convince him to get his butt off the couch and switch the TV from *Star Trek* to a Mutual of Omaha wildlife special on giraffes, since after all it is my birthday so I should decide what we watch, Fred calls out in a phony voice, "Children, please come into the kitchen."

"C'mon," I say to Mike. "It's show time."

We get up, turn off the TV, and go back to the kitchen, which is dark except for the light coming from the seventeen candles on top of my birthday cake (one for each year and one for good luck). I act all surprised like I'm supposed to even though I'm not, since this is what we do for birthdays every year, and then Fred and Shirley and Mike sing "Happy Birthday," which is a total disaster since everyone in my family, including me, is completely tone-deaf.

"Make a wish, Andrea," Shirley says, so I shut my eyes, wish that Frank and I will stay together forever, and blow. Then Shirley cuts a big piece of cake for Mike, a medium piece for me, and a tiny sliver for Fred. While we all munch away Shirley goes into the hall, and just as

Fred is sneaking himself another slice, she comes back with some envelopes and a box wrapped in shiny yellow paper.

"For me?" I ask, genuinely surprised. I thought I got my presents this morning.

"Well, if you don't want them, I'll take them," Mike says, motioning for Shirley to give the gifts to him.

"No way," I say, pushing aside my plate.

First I open an envelope from Shirley and Fred, which has another card in it, and tucked inside this one is a crisp one-hundred dollar bill. Next I open the card my grandmother sent from Florida. She sent some money too, so now I'm loaded.

"Your grandmother called while you and Mike were out," Shirley says. "You'll have to call her later and thank her."

"Okay," I say, reaching for the box. "Who can this be from?" I ask Mike, who just shrugs, so I know it's from him.

"Wow, this is cool," I say when I see what it is: a big coffee-table book about endangered animals, with really beautiful photos in it. I flip through the pages and almost start to cry because the animals are looking right out at the camera, and they look so sad, like they know their time is almost up, which just about breaks my heart.

"Thanks, everyone," I say, and just as I go back to my cake, the phone rings.

"I wonder who that's for," Fred says, like I'm the kind of teenage girl who gets phone calls every night. He answers the phone and then hands it to me. For a minute

I'm afraid it's Frank, but of course it can't be. He doesn't know my last name—or even my first name—for one thing. And for another thing, if a man ever called here asking for me, Fred would never just hand over the phone like that.

"Hello?"

"Hey, Andi, it's me. Ronnie. Happy birthday!"

"Ronnie!" I'm so happy to hear her voice. "How are you?"

"I'm pretty good. Hey, sorry I didn't send you a present or anything. I started making you a card, but then I got busy. . . ."

"Don't worry about it," I say. "What are you so busy with?"

"Oh you know, school and stuff. Hey, guess what, I made cheerleading."

"Cheerleading?" I say the word like I'm not sure what it means. "I thought you hated cheerleading."

"I never said I *hated* it, Andi," Ronnie says, which is such BS I almost puke up my birthday cake. Ronnie hates all that rah-rah, go-team, school-spirit stuff as much as I do. Or at least she used to.

"It's kind of cool, really," she goes on, and her voice is sincere, not sarcastic. "We have these really cute maroon and white uniforms and we get to travel with the team sometimes and . . ." Ronnie must realize from my silence that I'm in shock because she quickly changes the subject. "Anyway, never mind me, it's your birthday. So what's going on?"

"Oh, nothing much." What can I possibly tell Ronnie?

I can't talk to her about Frank with the Rents standing two feet away from me. I suppose I could take the call upstairs in the Units' bedroom, but all of a sudden, I don't really feel like talking to Ronnie. "Listen, I have to go, we're having a little celebration here. I'll call you soon, okay?" I hang up and go back to eating my birthday cake. When I finish, I ask Shirley for another piece, which she actually cuts and serves me without a nasty comment for once in her life, and then everyone goes upstairs to their separate rooms and my birthday party is over.

✖ ✖ ✖

It's Saturday morning, the day after my birthday, and everything's back to—and I use the word loosely— normal. Fred and I are eating bagels for breakfast and Shirley's chowing down on a Weight Watchers cheese Danish, which is really cottage cheese mixed with Sweet'n Low and cinnamon plopped on top of melba toast and broiled in the toaster oven. Gag me. Mike's gone already; Fred took him back to the airport early this morning. I wish he were still here so there'd at least be someone to talk to. Fred's knee-deep in *Newsday* and Shirley is skimming the recipes in *Good Housekeeping,* which is a pretty clear indication that no one's interested in having a conversation.

Shirley takes a last gulp of her coffee, puts her mug down, and, closing her magazine, gets up from the table. "Will you please clean up, Andrea," she says in a way that lets me know her words are a command, not a question. I guess now that my birthday's over, I'm back to being Cinderella.

Shirley and Fred wander off to watch television and have their after-breakfast smoke while I put all the left-over food into the refrigerator and load our plates into the dishwasher. When I'm done, I poke my head into the living room for a minute and stare at Superman as he flies across the TV screen.

When a commercial for Doublemint gum featuring two sets of identical twins comes on, I clear my throat. "I'm going to the library," I announce to the Rents, since I can't exactly tell them where I'm really going: to the store to buy some condoms.

"Want me to drive you?" Fred asks, half rising off the couch.

"Let your father take you, Andrea," Shirley chimes in. "It's awfully cold out."

"It's not that cold," I say quickly. "And besides, I could use the exercise."

"That's certainly true," says Shirley.

"Are you sure?" Fred asks with hope in his voice. "I feel like taking a little ride."

"I'm sure," I say, turning to go before he can join me.

Since it's all cloudy out and feels like it might snow, I put on my parka and head out to Jacoby's Drugs. I don't know where else to buy condoms, and I don't know if I'll even be able to buy them there. Mr. and Mrs. Jacoby both know me because their daughter, Horseface Hillary, is in my class, so what am I supposed to do, bring a box of them up to the back register where Mr. Jacoby works and say, "These are for my mother?" Yeah, right. Mrs. Jacoby usually works the front register and sometimes, like now during the holiday season, the Jacoby kids help out too: David, who's older than Mike and always wears this huge silver peace sign on a leather cord around his neck like he's stuck in the sixties; Steven, who graduated high school two years early because he's a total genius and is already in college so he probably won't be around; and of course my dear friend Horseface.

When I get to the drugstore I see good old Lucy ringing her Salvation Army bell out front like she does every year. Lucy's lived around here forever, and even though she's an adult, she has the intelligence of a child. No one knows her real name but everyone calls her Lucy because she has this beagle named Snoopy after Charlie Brown's dog in the Peanuts comic strip.

Usually Lucy spends her days walking up and down the street holding Snoopy in her arms, rocking him like a baby, poor puppy. Today, though, Snoopy is lying down by Lucy's feet because she can't hold him and ring her Salvation Army bell at the same time. And she is just ringing that bell like there's no tomorrow, let me tell you. She puts her whole arm and shoulder behind it. The problem, though, is that she rings her bell so loudly that no one will come near her to drop a quarter or two into her bucket. I don't know how Snoopy can stand it. You'd think Lucy would figure it out and let up a little, but like I already said, she's not the brightest bulb on the Christmas tree.

Well, I can't stand here forever trying to figure Lucy and Snoopy out, so I head into the drugstore. It's pretty crowded because there's only seven more shopping days left until Christmas, as it says on this gigantic banner hanging right over Lucy's head in front of the drugstore in case you happen to forget. And inside right when you walk in, there's this huge Christmas display of a cardboard Santa Claus holding a million candy canes, ten thousand tubes of red and green wrapping paper, and two hundred packages of tinsel, all next to a plastic reindeer with a blinking red nose. I pretend to be completely fascinated by all this, but what I'm really doing is casing the joint. And just as I suspected, Mr. Jacoby is manning the back register and Horseface Hillary is working up front with some girl I don't know. Mrs. Jacoby is nowhere in sight, but after a little detective work, I spot her in aisle fourteen. I walk past her trying to look like I know what I'm doing, because the last thing I want is Mrs. Jacoby saying, "Can I help you find something?" I suppose I could just casually say *Yes, the birth control, please,* like it's no big deal. Yeah, right.

I continue strolling around, looking up at the signs that say what's in each aisle. Aisle one: hair care. Aisle two: makeup. Aisle three: soap, deodorant, toothpaste. It doesn't say birth control or condoms or rubbers or raincoats anywhere, so I just start going up and down every aisle, browsing a little so I don't look like I'm loitering. Though anyone who really knows me would be suspicious immediately, because unlike the kind of girl you usually find in a drugstore, I'm not the hair-curling, mascara-wearing, nail-polishing type.

I head down the makeup aisle and pretend to look at

lipsticks with names like *Timeless Red* and *Endless Rose.*
Then I go down the next aisle and sniff some gross-
smelling bottles of perfume. After that I turn up the *fem-
inine hygiene* aisle which I walk through pretty quickly.
The next aisle brings me face to face with a hundred different kinds of aspirin: Bayer, St. Joseph, Excedrin—
just reading all the names is enough to give me a
headache. Then I round another corner and pass the vitamins section, the bandages section, and the foot-care
section, you know, the stuff to remove bunions and
corns and other gross things that grow on people's feet.
And then, right there next to the Dr. Scholl's Original
Foot Powder are condoms, condoms, condoms, as far as
the eye can see.

After looking up and down the aisle to make sure
the coast is clear, I step toward the display. Thank God
no one's around, but still, I have to be quick. But the
problem is, there's a million different brands. And
sizes. And guess what? There's no small. Just large and
extra large, I guess because most guys like to think their
thing is really big. I bet Frank thinks his is the size of
Yankee Stadium. I definitely better get extra large so I
don't insult him.

I just stand there for another minute trying to pick
out the best kind and finally decide to get some Trojans. I
reach out to grab a pack but before I can even get my
hands on one, I hear footsteps and guess who turns up
the aisle? Diane Carlson, of all people. With her mother.
Diane catches my eye and looks away fast, probably because she's totally mortified to be seen in public with a

parental unit. I take the opportunity to slide a few steps to my left and pick up a box of Band-Aids, which I study like it's the most interesting thing in the world.

"Ma, I don't need them," I hear Diane say behind me. "I'll be fine. It's just a little blister."

"If you didn't wear those ridiculous shoes," Mrs. Carlson says with a sigh. "Your feet are very important, Diane. If you don't take care of them now, you'll be sorry later on, believe me."

I look back over my shoulder and Diane rolls her eyes at me. I roll mine back in sympathy and Diane even gives me a little smile before she and her mother leave the aisle clutching Diane's blister remedy.

As soon as they leave, I sidestep back to the condoms, but then someone else comes up the aisle. Two women I don't know, thank God, but still, I have to wait it out while they discuss the merits of Flintstones vitamins versus some other brand. Finally, after an unbelievably long and boring conversation about how constipated vitamins make you, they leave empty-handed, and I scoot back down the aisle.

Finally I decide, what the heck, I'll just grab some. But then I have to figure out how many to get because they come in packs of different amounts: three, twelve, and thirty-six. Three doesn't sound like enough and thirty-six seems a little over the top. So I guess I'll get twelve. But they're kind of expensive. I guess I could ask Frank to give me money, but then again, I did just get all that birthday loot. See, things always work out one way or another. Except, stupid me, what am I thinking? I can't go up to the counter and pay for these like they're a box of Milk Duds. Old Horseface Hillary would spread this all over school in two seconds flat. What am I supposed to tell her, they're for a science project? No, I'm going to have to steal them.

This is a first-class, major problem, so if I'm going to rip off the raincoats, I better go for the package of thirty-six. Otherwise, if I get the twelve-pack, I'll just have to come back here in two weeks and steal more all over again.

Well, here goes nothing, I think, reaching out to grab a pack. But just as my hand makes contact, a voice whispers in my ear, "Get the lubricated. They work better." I drop the package fast and turn around just in time to see Diane Carlson disappear around the corner at the end of the aisle. Oh my God, I can't believe she saw me. My face is so hot, I'm sure it's as red as the suit the cardboard Santa Claus is wearing at the front of the store, and I can feel drops of sweat collecting under my armpits. Of all people, Diane Carlson. Well, at least she wasn't with Cheryl Healy when she saw me. Cheryl would probably find a way to sneak into the principal's office and broadcast this over the loudspeaker to the entire school during homeroom right after we say the Pledge of Allegiance. Diane isn't so bad. She doesn't have anything against me. I don't think. And she just gave me a little free advice, so maybe I don't have anything to worry about.

Well, what's done is done, I think as I take a package of Trojans and drop it into the pocket of my parka in one smooth motion. I wait a minute so I don't look too suspicious and then move up the aisle, stopping at the bandages again like I have all the time in the world.

On my way out of the store, I stop at the comic-book rack and pick up a *Mad* magazine with Alfred E. Neuman grinning on the cover, a thought bubble with the words *What—me worry?* hovering over his head. You'd think I'd be in a hurry to scram before I get busted and thrown in jail for shoplifting, but since I've been in here for a pretty long time, I figure it will look less suspicious if I buy something. So I take my reading material up to the cash register and hand it to good old Hillary, who pretends she doesn't even know me, like I care. I throw in a pack of Dentyne, hand her some dough, and wait for my change. And when Horseface hands it to me, she says, "Merry Christmas," which is completely stupid since we're both Jewish, and then finally I am out the door, safe and sound.

S-U-C-C-E-S-S, that's the way we spell success! Our school's stupid cheer goes round and round in my head for some reason as I stop to put my gloves on. Then before I head for home, I drop all the change I just got from Horseface Hillary into Lucy's Salvation Army bucket, and since I paid for my magazine and the gum with a twenty, it's definitely above and beyond the call of duty. But I don't care, since I just saved myself a mint on the condom caper. Just call me Andrea Robin Hood, I guess.

I bend down to scratch Snoopy between his poor, aching ears, and then, I don't know, the holiday spirit seizes me or something, because I straighten up and give

Lucy my gum and the *Mad* magazine without even thinking about it. And she's so surprised, she actually stops ringing her bell for a minute, which makes the street so quiet it's like everyone has gone completely deaf at the same time. Which is kind of creepy, like we've all just entered the Twilight Zone or something. But then Lucy starts up again, and everyone hurries away covering their ears, including me as I hustle my bustle home.

FOURTEEN

It starts the minute I walk into school, before I even have a chance to open my locker.

"Hey, Dee-Dee," Donald Caruso yells. "I'm writing a paper on the Trojan war and I hear you're an expert on Trojans. Can you help me out?"

Diane Carlson and her big fat mouth. I should have known she wouldn't keep what she saw to herself. I turn my back on Donald and open my locker without responding to him, but of course he doesn't let up. "Got a pair of rubbers in there?" he asks, peeking at the floor. "You never know when they might come in handy."

"Lay off, Donald," I say, slamming my locker shut.

"Lay?" he cracks up. "*Lay* off? God, Dee-Dee, is that all you ever think about? Man, I never knew you were such a sex maniac."

"Move aside," I say, elbowing him out of my way so I can get to homeroom.

"You don't have to knock me over with your knockers," he says, pretending to fall back. I give him the finger over my shoulder and round the corner.

"Blow me," Donald calls after me. God, can't he at least think of something original to say?

I could just kill Diane Carlson, but I know saying anything to her would just make it worse. The best I can do is avoid her and her crew all day, which I somehow manage to do, plus guard my knapsack with my life. I would die if anyone knew what I have in here, but luckily no one bothers to look. Donald teases me all day long, and when the last bell finally rings, I rush to my locker, grab my coat, and vacate the premises before he can start in again and I do something I know I'll regret.

As I walk down Farm Hill Road, I try to put it all out of my mind because I don't want to be in a bad mood when Frank gets here. He's exactly on time and boy, am I glad to see him.

"So, you think it's going to rain today, Vanessa?" Frank asks the minute I get into the car.

It would be a weird question if you didn't know what he meant because first of all, there's not a cloud in the sky, and second of all, it's only about thirty degrees out, so if anything was going to fall on our heads, it would definitely be snow. But Frank's not talking about the weather.

"I don't know, but I brought a raincoat just in case," I tell him, and Frank doesn't say anything but he smiles this smile—it's more like a grin, really—and my whole awful day at school just melts away. I'm so totally happy I feel like laughing or singing or, I don't know, rolling down my window and screaming my stupid head off.

Frank even starts whistling when we get out of the car and head up to the house. We go inside and I'm a little sad that my birthday decorations are gone but—get this—now there's a heater upstairs in the sleeping bag room. Oh sure, now that Frank's taking off his clothes too, we have a heater. Why couldn't we have one before, when it was just me freezing my butt off? I guess it doesn't really matter anymore, since the point is we finally have one. It works on kerosene, and it kind of smells, but I don't dare complain. Anyway, there's no electricity in the house, so I guess there's no other choice.

"So, let's see what you got." Frank turns on the heater and flops down right next to it on one of the sleeping bags. I flop down too and open my knapsack.

"Here." I hand him the package of Trojans.

Frank lets out a low whistle. "Wow, thirty-six. Somebody's prepared," he says, shaking the package a little. Then he opens the box and takes one out.

"Where'd you get these, anyway?" he asks.

"At the drugstore," I tell him, and then, like it's nothing, I add kind of proudly, "I stole them."

"You what?" Frank barks, like he's on the verge of getting mad. "Vanessa, what do you mean, you stole them?"

What do you mean, what do I mean? I want to ask him, and why is he getting so angry about it? "Well, I couldn't just go up to the cash register and pay for them, Frank. Mrs. Jacoby knows me, and I'm sure she'd tell my mother."

"Who's Mrs. Jacoby?" Frank asks, totally clueless.

"She owns the drugstore, Frank. *Jacoby's* Drugs?" God, doesn't he know anything? I decide to skip the part about being spotted by Diane Carlson since that probably wouldn't go over very well. "And anyway," I continue, "I thought you'd be really proud of me that I stole them, because now I'm risking going to jail to be with you, just like you are for me. So we're even."

"Stealing is a very serious thing, Vanessa," Frank says like he's a high school principal. "What do you want to do, end up in reform school?"

"But Frank, how else was I supposed to get them?" What I really want to say is *So why didn't* you *just get them?*

"Stolen goods." Frank looks over at the condoms and frowns. "I don't know if I can use them."

Oh for God's sake, give me a break. What do I have to do, attack the guy? What is Frank's problem? Maybe he's just scared. Yeah, I bet that's it. I make my voice all soft and soothing like he does when he knows I'm frightened. "C'mon now, Frank. Don't be mad. Let's just have a nice time together."

"You're sure you want to go through with this now, right, Vanessa?" Frank asks, like maybe he's changed his mind and wants to back out but doesn't want to admit it.

"Sure I'm sure, Frank. I want to make you happy. C'mere." I take his hand and pull him toward me, talking to him all the time like he's a scared puppy. "It's okay, Frank. It's all right. C'mon now. . . ."

"That's enough," Frank says, getting to his feet. He takes off his jacket and starts unbuttoning his shirt, and motions for me to do the same. Then he starts doing all the talking. "All right now, don't you ever forget this was all your idea, sweetheart. No one's forcing you into anything here, remember that. This is your choice."

I don't say anything and the house is so quiet you could hear a condom drop. Frank turns his back to me for a minute and then turns back around and says, "Lie down," like he's talking to a dog, so I do.

I close my eyes and in one second Frank is on top of me, which feels like I'm being crushed to death, but before I have a chance to say anything, like "Get off," we're actually doing it.

"Ow!" I yell, because it really hurts, but Frank tells me to shut up so I do. I can't even believe I couldn't wait to do this. How can this be the huge deal that everyone makes such a big gigantic fuss about?

I keep my eyes shut until it's over, and when it finally is, I have to wait for Frank to get off me, which takes a while because first he has to lie there panting like he just ran the New York City Marathon. Though from the way he was hyperventilating two seconds ago, I could have sworn he was having a heart attack.

When Frank's breathing gets back to normal, he whispers in my ear, "So, Vanessa was it everything you thought it would be?"

"Oh no, Frank, it was much, much more," I tell him in this mushy voice, and Frank's so dumb, he doesn't even get that I'm being totally sarcastic. He just smiles, pushes himself off, and says, "Let's go," like all of a sudden he's in a hurry. I feel like asking, *What's the rush, got a date?* but of course I know he doesn't.

I sit up, throw the package of Trojans into my knapsack, and pick up my clothes, but I feel so gross I can't even stand the thought of putting them on.

"Get a move on, kiddo," Frank says, slapping my behind. He's got everything on already except his shoes and his jacket, so I hurry and put on my clothes too. When I'm all dressed, he says, "C'mere," like he wants to hold me for a minute, and even though I don't want to, I let him give me a hug.

"So how does it feel to be a real woman?" he asks.

"Terrific," I say, even though it isn't true. But I don't know, maybe it'll get better. They say the first time is never that hot and you have to communicate with your partner so he learns what you like. That's what all the magazine articles say, anyway. Yeah, right. Frank happens to know exactly what I like. He knows how to make me feel good. When he wants to.

Maybe it was his turn to feel good today. Maybe we'll take turns from now on. That's only fair, I guess.

Frank gives me a big hug and kiss and then lets go of me and heads downstairs. I grab my knapsack and go after him, and then we get in the car and drive back to the spot where he drops me off. As usual, I know better than to ask if I'll see him tomorrow, and to tell you the truth, I don't know if I even want to. But Frank's got other plans.

"Tomorrow," he reminds me, squeezing my knee. "Be there or be square." But instead of feeling happy, I just feel like taking the stupid screwdriver he uses to start the car off his dashboard and stabbing him with it, I really do. God, I wish I could figure out what is wrong with me. But I can't, so there's nothing to do but get out of the car, and the second I do, Frank gives his usual wave and just starts driving away.

I plod along thinking about how today was supposed to be the best day of my entire life and it turned out to be nothing but a great big fat disappointment. I mean, Frank could even go to jail for what we did, so you'd think it would be absolutely, positively, I don't know, *spectacular* or something, but it wasn't. At least not in my opinion. Which obviously means there's something seriously wrong with me. Like that's a big surprise.

When I turn the corner onto my block, I see that Shirley's car is missing in action, so at least one thing is going my way today. My grandmother always says you should be grateful for the little things in life and I guess she's right because I don't feel like talking to anyone right now. Especially Shirley. What I really feel like doing is taking a scalding hot shower, putting on my pajamas, and getting into bed with Snowball and my other stuffed animals and just pulling the covers over my head. So I do.

About an hour later, I hear the front door open, which means Shirley's home. Eventually she notices I haven't started making Fred's supper yet and she comes upstairs to find me.

"What are you doing in bed?" she asks, standing in the doorway to my room.

"I don't feel so good," I say, which at this point is totally true.

"What's the matter? Do you have a headache?"

"Yeah," I say, since that's easier than making something up. "I think it's because of my period." *Good cover, Andi,* I tell myself, because now if Shirley goes into the bathroom and sees my washed-out underwear hanging in the shower, she won't be suspicious.

"I'll get you some aspirin," Shirley says, and then she disappears. *Just bring me the whole bottle,* I think, since I wouldn't mind taking about fifty right now, but she only brings me two.

"Here." Shirley hands me two aspirin tablets and a Porky Pig glass filled with ginger ale. I decide not to take her glass selection personally, even though I probably should. Then Shirley actually sits on the edge of my bed for a minute and feels my forehead with the back of her hand. "I don't think you have a fever," she says, like she would know. Then she takes my empty glass and gets up to leave.

"Shirley, can you stay with me a little?"

My mother stops halfway between standing up and sitting down and gives me this puzzled look, like I just spoke to her in Japanese. I don't even know why I said it. I guess I don't feel like being alone. Shirley sits back down again, but she stays perched on the edge of the bed, like a cat that wants to step on the branch of a tree but isn't sure if it's strong enough to support its weight.

After a minute, Shirley sits back, crosses her legs, and starts picking at the fuzz on my bedspread. She's nervous because she can't go for more than a minute without a cigarette and she knows I'll have a major fit if she even thinks about smoking in here. She looks out my window and sighs this big heavy sigh but she doesn't say anything. Clearly, if we're going to talk, it's up to me to begin. I wish Shirley would just read some *Winnie-the-Pooh* to me, but I'm too old to ask for that.

"Shirley, how did you know that Daddy was the right one?" I ask, and I don't know who's more surprised to hear the word *Daddy* fly out of my mouth, Shirley or me, since I've been calling my father Fred since I was twelve.

She looks at me and shrugs. "I don't know, Andrea. You just know these things."

"But how?" I ask. "I mean, do you believe in fate?"

"I don't know, Andrea," she says again. "I suppose certain things are just meant to be."

"Tell me how you met," I say.

"Oh, Andrea, you've heard this story a hundred times."

"Tell me anyway."

"Why?"

"Because."

"Oh, all right," she says with another sigh. Then she looks out the window again. "I was sixteen and your father was seventeen. You know he was an excellent swimmer when he was young. He was very handsome, with very broad shoulders. All the girls noticed him. Then one day I was at the pool, and your father was swimming laps. I guess he got a little carried away with himself and lost his focus, because he got to the end of the lane, smacked into the wall, and practically knocked himself silly."

"Were his eyes as bad then as they are now?" I ask since my father is legally blind when he's not wearing his glasses.

"Oh yes," Shirley says. "Though they weren't so bad that he didn't notice me, even though he was only half conscious," she says with pride. "I was wearing a white bathing suit that was cut like this." Shirley makes a heart shape with both hands over her chest. "I wish I still had that suit. It was very flattering. Your father used to say I looked like Elizabeth Taylor in it." She stares out the window again with this dreamy look in her eyes and then snaps out of it. "Where was I?"

"At the pool with Fred half conscious."

"And bleeding, too. So I brought him a towel and he looked up and saw me all in white and said, 'Where did this angel come from?' And that was that. We've been together ever since."

"You forgot something."

"What?" Shirley asks, making it clear her patience is running out.

"You forgot to say the part about how his legs were so thin his friends used to call him Freddie Spaghetti."

"Oh, right. Though now with his potbelly, they'd probably call him Freddie Meatball."

"Freddie Meatball?" Shirley has never said anything like that before and it strikes me so funny, I giggle until I get hysterical. "Freddie Meatball? *Freddie Meatball?*" I shriek, and then I'm laughing so hard tears pour from my eyes. A minute later I really am crying, but I'm still laughing too, and I can't get hold of myself.

"Andrea, are you all right?" Shirley asks, frowning.

God, what does she think? I give up and just tell her what she so obviously wants to hear. "I'm fine, Shirley. Just fine. You're dismissed."

Shirley practically jumps off the bed, and then, not wanting to look too eager to leave, asks me if I need anything. I shake my head and wave my hand in front of my face like I'm shooing away a fly. She takes the hint and I lie there listening to her shuffle through the hall and down the stairs to the living room. Her footsteps get softer and softer and when I can't hear them anymore, I pull the covers over my head and shut my eyes and for some reason that makes me feel like I'm lying in a coffin. So I keep really still and pretend I'm dead, which actually doesn't sound half bad at the moment.

I don't know if anyone would even care if I died. Mike would, I guess, but he's probably halfway to Hawaii by now. Fred would stay home from the office for a day or two, just because it would look weird if he didn't. And Shirley? She couldn't care less about what happens to me. She'd probably just pop a few extra happy pills, go to her figure salon more, and be glad no one was around to give her grief about her cigarettes. I wonder if Ronnie would come in from Pennsylvania for my funeral. Probably. And I guess my grandmother would fly up from Florida.

And what about Frank? Would he come? How would

he even know? What if somehow he did show up and Shirley asked him, *Are you a friend of Andrea's?* He'd say, *Andrea? I thought her name was Vanessa.* And then he'd be so mad I lied to him he'd kill me, except I'd be dead already so he couldn't.

I wonder what Frank would do if I didn't show up tomorrow. Would he come looking for me? I mean, maybe I really am sick. But if I don't go to school tomorrow, I'll really screw things up on account of finals. No, I have to go. And maybe Frank will be back to his old self tomorrow. I'm sure he will; his bad moods never last two days in a row. Maybe he just got so excited that we finally got to go all the way that he just lost control of himself. Yeah, I'm sure that's it. I'm sure once he gets used to the fact that he can do anything he wants to me whenever he feels like it, everything will be just fine.

FIFTEEN

"Frank, can we talk?"

"Talk, Vanessa?" he says, like I just asked if we could do something ridiculous, like rob a bank.

We're upstairs in the sleeping bag room, and I don't know, I guess Frank thought we'd just dash upstairs, whip off our clothes, and do the same thing we did yesterday. He didn't even smoke a cigarette or tell me to put on an outfit.

"Frank." I stare down at the tip of his work boot, because I know if I look up I'll cry. "I don't know, Frank. I . . . I didn't have such a good time yesterday."

There. I said it. I keep looking down at Frank's boot,

which doesn't move, and wait for him to say something. He doesn't for a long time. Finally I look up into his eyes, which are dark with anger, and I'm afraid he's going to start yelling at me, but he doesn't. In fact, he doesn't say anything, which feels even worse for some reason.

"I don't know, I guess there's something wrong with me because . . ." I swallow hard and speak so softly I can hardly hear myself. "Because I liked it better before we went all the way."

Frank sighs, like he can't believe what an idiot he has for a girlfriend, and then he fishes around in his jacket for a cigarette, which means I've got a little time, since we can't exactly do it while he's smoking. Maybe we won't have to do it at all today. Which would be fine with me.

"Now you listen to me, little girl," Frank says in a voice that lets me know I'm not going to like whatever he's about to say. "For months I've been hearing 'I want to make *you* happy, Frank.' And then the first time we do something that makes me happy, this is what I get."

I don't know what to say, so I just keep mum and stare at the floor.

"What were you, lying to me, Vanessa? When you said you wanted to make me feel good, obviously you didn't mean it."

"Frank, that's not true. You know I'd never lie to you." I look up but it's hard to meet his eyes, since I have lied to him, and I'm still lying to him, since I don't have the guts to tell him my name isn't Vanessa.

"You know what, Vanessa?" Frank asks, striking a

match to light his cigarette. "What we do here isn't about you anymore, you got that? From now on, it's about me."

"Isn't it about both of us, Frank?" I ask. "Can't we, like, take turns or something?"

"Turns?" Frank pitches his cigarette on the floor and stubs it out even though he's only taken one drag from it. "What do you think this is, Parcheesi?"

"Well, can't you just go a little slower?"

"I'll go slow, all right," Frank says. Then he lunges at me and grabs me hard, right through my jacket.

"Ow! Cut it out." I back away from him, but he follows and pins me to the wall.

"Listen, you fat little tramp . . ."

"I'm not fat," I say, even though I am. "And I'm not a tramp. Frank, what is with you today?" I try to get away from him, but it's like I'm a glob of peanut butter and Frank and the wall are bread.

"Relax, Vanessa. C'mon now." Frank softens his voice and touches me gently, the way he knows I like. "Let's just have a good time together, okay?"

"Okay," I say, even though I don't feel like it.

"That's it, Vanessa, just relax now," Frank says, and as soon as I start to, his voice changes. "Listen, Vanessa," he hisses in my ear. "You're spoiled now. Used goods. No one else will ever want you. You're mine now, and you'll do exactly what I say."

"I think I want to go home, Frank," I whisper, because my voice is stuck somewhere down in my throat.

"I don't really care what you want," Frank says. I start to cry, but Frank doesn't do anything, so it's true: he doesn't really care. Then I hear something that makes my skin crawl: Frank's zipper being unzipped. He can't be serious.

"Frank, I don't want to . . ."

"I don't really care what you want."

"But Frank—"

"Shut up."

"But—"

"I said, shut *up*."

"But—"

"Vanessa, if you don't do what I say by the count of three, you're really going to be sorry. One . . . two . . ."

"All right, all right." I bend down to undo my sneakers, unlacing them very slowly, stalling for time. This is really scary. Frank's been nasty before, but never this mean. This is *mean* mean. I guess I could try and make a run for it, but I'm not exactly in marathon shape here.

"Get down." Frank points to the sleeping bags even though I'm still dressed.

"Frank, I don't want to. . . ."

"Will you shut your trap?" he says, grabbing my arm and pulling it until I'm forced to get down on my knees.

I start to stand up, but Frank pushes me back down. "Not so fast, sister," he says.

And then he makes me do something, something that makes what we did yesterday look like a walk in the park. And I want to die, I really do. When it's over, I'm in total shock, I really am. I try not to cry, but I can't help it; the tears just drip down my face while Frank gets dressed and doesn't even notice.

"C'mon, let's go," Frank says, and I can't believe he thinks I'm just going to hop in his car like nothing unusual happened today. Then again, what choice do I have?

Frank picks up his jacket and makes his way downstairs, but then I hear his footsteps stop before he opens the front door. "Vanessa," he calls up, "you have exactly one minute to get your butt down here. Otherwise, I'm leaving without you."

I don't think Frank would really do that, but just in case, I stand up and race downstairs.

"Fifty-eight, fifty-nine, sixty," Frank counts, looking at his watch. "You're really pushing it, little girl." We get into the car and I sit as far away from Frank as possible, which isn't very far since this is hardly a Cadillac.

Frank starts the car, and when he jams the screwdriver into the ignition, all I can think about is something else jamming into me, and then I can't help it, my whole body starts to shake. My teeth are even chattering and everything. You'd think Frank would notice and say something, like *Are you chilly, Vanessa?* or *Are you freaked out, Vanessa?* or even *Are you having a bad LSD trip, Vanessa?* But all he does is look out the window and drive. So I look out the window too. And then, right after we go through a yellow light, all of a sudden, out of nowhere, a squirrel darts into the road.

"Frank, look out!" I yell, but he ignores me, so I lunge for the wheel and pull it to the right.

"What are you, crazy?" Frank elbows me out of the way and swerves the car back over to the left and that's when I feel us go over this bump and I hear the thud. The awful, awful thud, which is absolutely the most horrible sound I've ever heard in my entire life.

"Stop the car! Stop the car!" I grab for the wheel again, but Frank pushes me back in my seat. So I just start screaming and screaming until Frank has no choice: he either has to stop the car or have his eardrums shattered. As soon as he pulls over, I jump out of the car and run back to where the squirrel was, but it's all over. The poor thing is dead and it's all my fault. If I hadn't gone for the steering wheel, Frank wouldn't have had to swerve and the squirrel would probably have made it across the road just fine. But now it's dead. Like I wish I was.

I don't know how long I stand there and I don't even hear when Frank comes up behind me. All I hear is some idiot shrieking her stupid head off, louder and louder and louder, and until Frank spins me around and shakes me by the shoulders, I don't even realize it's me.

"Stop it, Vanessa," he yells. "Stop it." I shut my mouth, and the screaming ceases, but then the tears start falling. "C'mon now, there's nothing we can do. Get back in the car."

"No." I stomp my foot like a two-year-old.

"Vanessa, c'mon, I have to go." Frank looks up and down the road and all of a sudden I realize he's afraid someone will see us. *Good,* I think. *Let them.*

"Do you want me to leave without you?" Frank asks. When I don't answer, he says, "I'm leaving," like he's my father trying to call my bluff and I'm some stupid little kid who won't stop playing with her toys even though it's time to go.

"You would leave, wouldn't you?" My words come out all choppy because I'm still crying. "You'd just leave me here on the side of the road, like a . . . like a dead squirrel." Then I collapse in his arms, bury my face in his jacket, and just start sobbing all over the place. Frank holds me, but I can feel he's all jumpy about this, and in fact a few cars do go by, but I'm sure they can't tell from the back of my head that I'm under seventeen. And even if they can, who cares?

Finally I calm down enough to catch my breath, and Frank takes my hand and leads me back to the car. But I won't get in. "We can't just leave it in the middle of the road, Frank."

"What do you want to do with it?" he asks in a voice that lets me know he's had just about enough.

"We have to bury it."

"Will you just get in the car, Vanessa?" Frank rubs his forehead with one hand.

"No, Frank, I won't." He glares at me and starts to open his door, but I beat him to it by yanking open my door first, and grabbing his screwdriver. "We have to bury the squirrel."

Frank stares at me but I hold my ground until he starts walking back to where the squirrel is. I follow him and we find two sticks to dig a hole with. It isn't very deep but it's the best we can do. Thank God it's warmed up a little and the snow's started to melt so the ground is soggy instead of frozen.

Frank puts the squirrel into its grave and I stand there and just look at it for a minute. It's lying on its side and I stare at its eye, which is still open. The squirrel looks shocked, like it can't believe what just happened to it. I can't believe it either.

I cover the squirrel with some dirt and some leaves, and then just stand there for a minute, wishing I knew how to say Kaddish, which is the Jewish prayer for the dead. But I don't know the words, so I just stare down at the squirrel's grave silently with Frank standing next to me. And then, just as we turn to get back in the Volkswagen, I hear a car slow down and a voice chant out the window:

"Dee-Dee and her boyfriend sittin' in a tree.
K-I-S-S-I-N-G.
First comes love
Then comes marriage
Then comes Dee-Dee with a baby carriage."

Donald—I know it's Donald, since he recently got his license and he's the only one who ever calls me Dee-Dee—puts the pedal to the metal and peels out, laughing like a maniac. Frank stands absolutely still like he's in shock, but I think fast.

"That was weird, huh?" I say. "I must look like some girl named Dee-Dee from the back."

"Let's go," Frank says in a stage whisper, which is weird since now there's no one around to hear us. I fork over his stupid screwdriver so he can start his car and get us out of there. We drive for a few minutes and then Frank actually asks me if I'm all right.

"No, Frank, I'm not all right," I say. "I don't know, I don't think I want to see you for a while."

"Listen, Vanessa." Frank takes his eyes off the road for a split second to glare at me. "Just shut up and behave yourself."

"You can't make me come here."

"I can't?" Frank lets out a big sigh. "Do you ever want to see your mother's wedding ring again?"

"I don't care about her stupid ring," I say, which is totally not true and he knows it. "Besides," I go on, "you promised you'd give it back to me when I'm seventeen. You said."

"Don't whine." Frank turns onto Farm Hill Road and pulls over to the fence. "If you don't care about your mother's ring, maybe you'll care about a certain roll of film I have in my possession."

"What film?"

"A roll of pictures of a certain girl wearing, well, she wasn't wearing very much, now, was she?"

The pictures . . . I forgot about the pictures. God, how stupid can a person be? *Can't a guy have a picture of his own girlfriend? Don't you trust me?* God, I am such an idiot.

"Hmm. I could make a few hundred copies and tape them to everyone's lockers at your school," Frank says, like he's thinking out loud.

I feel sick, really sick. My stomach is clenched so tight it feels like it's inside out. "You don't even know where I go to school," I say, trying to keep my voice steady.

"Good old Greenwood High. Home of the infamous Greenwood Woodpeckers," Frank says, and for some reason it really upsets me that he knows the name of our stupid football team. "Go, Peckers, go! Go, Peckers, go!" Frank cheers with one fist in the air, then lets out this really mean laugh. "I know all about you, Vanessa." Frank draws out the word *Vanessa* in a way that makes me think he knows it isn't my real name. "I know where you live, I know what classes you take. . . ."

"You do not!"

"How do you know what I know and what I don't know?" he asks. I start to cry again, but Frank couldn't care less. "Don't you get any big ideas in that little head of yours about not showing up tomorrow, you hear me?"

"Yes," I say in a tiny voice.

"Yes, what?"

"Yes, Frank."

"Good. I'm glad we understand each other, Vanessa. See you tomorrow." And then before I can even get my car door open, Frank leans over and kisses me. Hard. On the mouth. I try to pull away but he shoves his tongue between my lips and moves it around like a big fat worm. If I had any guts at all, which obviously I don't, I would just bite it off. But I'm such a wimp I'm never going to tell on Frank, and he knows it. Frank's right. I belong to him now, just like he said. I'm spoiled. Used goods. No one will ever want me after what happened today. Not that it matters, since nobody ever wanted me before, anyway.

SIXTEEN

Today I just couldn't take school anymore, so I cut out early and came down to stand by the fence and wait for Frank. I was hoping Bessie would be out so I could talk to her, but she isn't, so I'm just standing here tearing at my split ends and thinking things over. Like maybe I should run away. From Frank, from Fred and Shirley, from everything. Just think what it would be like to never see Donald Caruso ever again. I was pretty nervous about seeing him after what happened yesterday, but luckily he was absent. It's the last day before vacation, so a lot of kids didn't bother coming to school.

Anyway, if I did run away, how far would I get? I

don't have a lot of money besides my birthday loot, which isn't all that much. I guess I could get more loot by raiding Shirley's pocketbook. It's always on the kitchen counter, so it wouldn't be so hard to empty her wallet while she's in the living room watching one of her soap operas. Not that I want to steal from my own mother. That's much worse than shoplifting, even I know that. I could always pay her back later, I guess. So it would be more like borrowing.

But where would I go? Maybe into the city. It's pretty easy to get lost in the crowd in New York, but where would I sleep? Like I said, I only have a little over a hundred dollars, and even if I do take money from Shirley, it's not like she keeps a small fortune in her purse or anything; it's more like fifty or sixty bucks.

Maybe I could take a bus up to Mike's school. I'm sure he'd help me figure something out. Maybe he'd even let me go to Hawaii with him if he hasn't left already. I know just as much about picking avocados as he does. And I wouldn't get in his way; I wouldn't even say anything about him selling dope. I don't know, though. I'm sure Mike doesn't want his stupid baby sister tagging along all over the place, spoiling his fun. Though I don't know how much fun it would be anyway, with Mike being stoned out of his gourd all the time. I don't know, wasting your life by being wasted every single second doesn't really appeal to me.

I flip my hair over my shoulder so I won't totally destroy it and start pacing up and down the road. I heard somewhere that pacing helps you figure things out. But it doesn't work for me: I just can't think of anything to do but wait for Frank.

By now you probably think I'm not playing with a full deck here, and in a way you're probably right. Only a complete nut job would keep seeing Frank after what he did yesterday. Or maybe you think I'm too scared not to show up, but that's not it either. You see, the thing is I *want* to see him again. Why? Well, first of all, if you have to ask the question, you won't understand the answer. Love can't be explained. It doesn't make sense, it's just how you feel. And second of all, everyone's entitled to a bad day every now and then. And Frank's no exception.

I don't know why I don't like going all the way with him or doing what I did yesterday, which is supposed to be every guy's favorite thing in the world, so most girls must like doing it, or at least get used to it. There must be something really wrong with me. Maybe I'll figure it out over Christmas vacation. After today I won't see Frank for eleven whole days, which to tell you the truth is kind of a relief. I haven't told Frank yet that we don't have school until January third. I'll have to tell him today. I hope he doesn't say I have to meet him anyway, because it'll be hard to sneak away from the house when there's no school. This library excuse can only go so far.

In the middle of having all these thoughts, I hear Frank's car, so I take a deep breath to pull myself together, and then hop into the Volkswagen as soon as it stops. Frank's quiet all the way to the house, which is fine with me. When we pass the place where we hit the squirrel yesterday, I try not to look but I can't help it, and a lump forms in my throat when I see the little pile of leaves we put over it. I try to swallow the lump but it gets stuck halfway and turns into a kind of sob. Frank puts his hand on my knee and pats it a few times, which shocks me, since I didn't think he cared. Which is a terrible thing for a girl to think about her boyfriend, so I'm glad it isn't true.

When we get to the house, Frank says, "Go upstairs," which is what I used to do before we went all the way, so maybe the old Frank is back and things will be normal again.

"Do you want me to put on an outfit?" I ask.

"What? Sure," he says, but I can tell he's distracted by something, though I have no idea what. It seems like part of him is here and part of him is far away.

"What's the matter, Frank?"

He doesn't bother answering me, which makes me sad. I wish Frank would open up to me and tell me his problems, but he probably thinks I'm just a stupid sixteen-year-old kid who wouldn't understand. Or maybe he didn't hear me.

"Frank, is something the matter?"

"No, Vanessa. Just go upstairs."

I climb the steps slowly, go into my dressing room, and reach into the closet for an outfit, any outfit, I don't care which one. It turns out to be the very first outfit Frank bought me—the black lacy one—which doesn't quite hide my big fat thighs, but Frank really likes it. Or at least he used to.

When I'm all ready, I go into the sleeping bag room,

sit down, and wait for him. I try not to feel afraid of him, and maybe I don't have to be, since he seems like he's in a better mood today, but you never know with Frank. While I'm waiting, I take a few deep breaths and try to relax and hope for the best. "You're such a pessimist, Andrea," Shirley always says to me. "Can't you look on the bright side for a change?" And even though I totally hate doing anything Shirley says, she's not around at the moment, so that's what I do.

And sure enough, a minute later Frank walks in with this great big smile on his face like he's actually happy to see me. I smile back and then, out of nowhere, my body starts to shake. I try to stop it so Frank won't see, but I can't control it.

"You look so beautiful," Frank says, licking his lips like I'm a great big piece of birthday cake. "I've been looking forward to seeing you all day."

"You have?" I can't believe it. The old Frank *is* back.

"Of course I have." He takes off his jacket and drapes it over my shoulders. It smells like cigarettes. "Are you cold, baby?" he asks. Then he drops down next to me. "Who wouldn't look forward to spending the afternoon with a beautiful woman like you?" he asks, opening up his arms.

Frank gathers me up and starts kissing my face all over, my eyes, my nose, my cheeks, my mouth, my chin, even my forehead, like I'm the most precious thing in the world.

"Vanessa," he says softly. "My beautiful, beautiful Vanessa." I feel so happy being with him like this, I could just purr. Frank holds me close, and the whole time he's touching me, he keeps telling me how beautiful I am, how special I am, how wonderful I am. I feel like I'm floating through a dream and the past two days were just a nightmare that is finally, finally over. This is exactly the way it's supposed to be. Frank is so sweet and kind and gentle, like, I don't know, some guy in a movie or something. I'm so happy I let out a deep sigh, and then try to stifle it, because I don't want to do something that might make him mad. I don't want to spoil this moment for anything.

Frank smiles at me and then lies down and pulls me beside him. I try not to stiffen up but I can't help it, and I'm afraid Frank is going to get mad, but he doesn't.

"Shh, Vanessa," he says, "relax. I'm not going to hurt you. All I want to do is hold you." And I'm so relieved to hear that, and so happy that Frank's being so nice to me, I just start crying my eyes out.

"Vanessa, I'm sorry for being such a selfish prick yesterday," he says. "Please stop crying. It'll never happen again. I promise."

"Cross your heart and hope to die?" I sniffle.

"Cross my heart and hope to die," he says. "C'mon. Everything's all right now, isn't it? We're together, and that's all that counts." Then Frank wraps his arms around me even tighter and rocks me back and forth, but it still takes a while for me to stop with the waterworks.

"There, that's better," he says when I finally do.

"I have something to tell you," I mumble into Frank's arm.

"I can't hear you, sweetheart."

"I said I have something to tell you." I lift my head up. "I can't . . . I can't . . ." Just the thought of it makes me almost start crying again. "I can't see you for eleven days, Frank. Today was the last day of school before Christmas vacation and we don't go back until January third."

"That stinks," Frank says. He sits up and pulls on his shirt. "Go get dressed, Vanessa."

"Are you mad?" I ask in this tiny voice that's almost a whimper.

"No," he says, "it's not your fault. I'll think of something."

I go into the other room and get dressed, wondering what Frank is thinking. I don't have to wait long.

"Vanessa, this is really stupid," Frank says, leaning against the doorjamb, smoking a cigarette. For a minute I think he means my using this room to change my clothes in is really stupid, but that's not what he means at all. "I don't know if I can take being without you for eleven days," he says.

"Well, what do you think we should do?" I ask him.

"I think we should run away."

"Really?" I race over to him and throw myself in his arms. "Really? Really?"

"Take it easy, baby," Frank says, holding his cigarette out of the way so he doesn't set my hair on fire. He flings it on the ground and stubs it out with his boot, and then all of a sudden he's laughing and hugging me and kissing me. "Are you sure you want to go away with your old uncle Frank?"

"Yes!" I practically scream into his eardrum. "Yes, yes, yes!" Oh my God, I can't believe this is happening. "Where will we go, Frank? New York?"

"New York? You mean Manhattan?"

I nod.

"Nah," Frank says. "That's too close to home. I think we have to head south. Like ducks for the winter."

"South? Where in the south?"

Frank motions for me to put on my coat and we head downstairs, still talking about our plans. "Georgia, maybe. Or Mississippi," he says, and the way he says it, it's more like he's thinking out loud than talking to me.

"Why there?" I ask, getting into the car.

Frank doesn't start it up right away. "Vanessa, they're much more liberal down south when it comes to relationships between older men and younger women. The laws aren't so strict. We could even get married."

Married! I'm so shocked, I'm speechless, and I don't say anything while Frank starts the car. We stay quiet most of the way back, but it's a good kind of quiet, a happy kind of quiet, if you know what I mean.

When Frank pulls over, I don't want to get out of the car. "Maybe we should leave right now," I tell him. "I don't need anything from my house."

"Vanessa, let's not be hasty," Frank says, and my stomach freezes because I'm scared he's changing his mind. "I want you to think this over very carefully. You can tell me your answer after Christmas vacation, and if you still want to go, we'll leave on January third, when I pick you up after school."

"But Frank, I don't have to think about it," I say, and then lower my voice because I'm starting to whine.

"Yes, you do. You need to think about it very carefully. Every choice you make has consequences. You never know what life has in store for you," Frank says, which is totally true. I certainly didn't know life had *him* in store for me. "Now give me a kiss to last eleven days." He leans in toward me and we kiss for a little while, and then I have to go. And I almost don't mind because I float like a cloud all the way home.

SEVENTEEN

It's only the beginning of vacation and I'm already jump-ing out of my skin. I'm so bored being home with noth-ing to do and so happy about running away with Frank, I can hardly sit still. I want to do all those ridiculous, corny things that people in love do—you know, shout it from the rooftops and whatever. Believe it or not, I was in such a good mood when I woke up this morning, I actu-ally volunteered to go grocery shopping with Shirley. When we got back, I even unloaded the car for her, but I forgot to tell her that one of her cans of Tab had fallen out of the bag and had spent the entire drive home rolling around on the floor. Of course that was the can Shirley picked to open, and when she popped the top, it exploded all over the place. I cleaned it up and told her I was sorry a million times, but I didn't tell her that I feel just like that pink can of Tab: *spewing* with excitement.

After the soda fiasco, Shirley left to go to her figure salon and I came up here to sit in Mike's room and think about things. I wish Mike were home so I could tell him about Frank. He's the only one who would totally understand how happy I am to finally be getting out of Greenwood once and for all.

The phone rings and I jump off Mike's bed to run into the Rents' room and get it. I don't know why I'm in such a rush since it's never for me. But before I can grab the receiver, I hear Fred saying hello downstairs. He's home all this week too, and he's just as bored as I am.

After a minute, Fred raises his voice. "What? You get on the next plane and get your butt home right now before I drive up to Buffalo and get you," I hear him say, which can only mean one thing: he's talking to Mike. So I pick up the upstairs extension as quietly as I can and listen in.

"I'll just be here a few more days," Mike says. "I'm going skiing with some friends."

Skiing? Yeah, right. Mike's about as athletic as I am.

"Michael Kaplan, now you listen to me. . . ."

"I have to go. Say hi to Mom and Squirt," Mike says, and then hangs up the phone. I hang up too and go downstairs to see what Fred's going to do. He's staring at the phone in the kitchen as though it has something more to tell him.

"That was your brother," Fred informs me. "Has he ever said anything to you about going skiing?"

"Skiing?" I pretend to ponder it. "I'm not sure."

"Your brother's up to something," Fred says, taking off his glasses and rubbing his eyes. "You sure you don't know anything about this little skiing vacation of his?"

"I'm sure," I say, which is actually true. I mean, you can't exactly go skiing in Hawaii. I go back upstairs before Fred can ask me any more questions about Mike. I wonder where he is and why he even called. I'm sure he's not still in Buffalo. He's probably on the road somewhere on his hitchhiking adventure.

The next day Mike calls again, but this time I answer the phone.

"Mike, how are you? Where are you?" I ask.

"Shh, Squirt, don't use my name. I don't want the Rents to know I'm calling."

"Don't worry," I tell him. "I'm upstairs in their bedroom and they're down in the living room watching TV."

"Good. Now listen, Squirt, I need you to do me a favor."

"What?"

"I need some cash, you know what I'm saying? I got kicked off the highway yesterday and left my dope behind—"

"In the Coke can?"

"Yeah, in the Coke can. After this cop made me get off the entry ramp to the highway, I waited like ten minutes and then went back to get it, but he was still there on the lookout for me, so I had to keep moving. I need to score bad, man, I haven't gotten high in like two days. Let me tell you, dope is a lot more expensive out here than it is back home."

"Out where?" I ask. "Mike, where are you?"

"Colorado."

"Colorado?" Fred and I say at the same time. Uh-oh. He must have picked up the downstairs extension to see who called and when he heard the voices of his darling children decided to listen in.

"Mike," Fred says, and I can tell he's trying to control his temper. "What are you doing in Colorado? And don't give me any BS about going skiing."

"I'm on my way to Hawaii, Pops," Mike says, his voice remaining calm. I guess he figures Fred can't really do anything to him since he's two thousand miles away.

"Hawaii?" Fred screams. "*Hawaii?* Now you listen to me, Michael Kaplan. I didn't work my butt off for all these years so some lousy kid of mine could run off to a luau. Is that clear?"

"Clear as a bell," Mike says, and the calmer he is, the more agitated Fred gets.

"All right, mister. Fine. Just send me your address so I can send you your bill.

"Bill? What bill?" Mike asks.

"What bill?" Fred asks back. "Food, clothing, tuition. And that's just for starters. You waste your own hard-earned money, not mine." Fred slams down the phone and I hang up a minute later.

"Andrea, get down here," Fred bellows from the kitchen.

I take a deep breath and head downstairs. Fred is slumped in a chair at the table with his head in his hands.

"What do you know about your brother going to Hawaii?" he asks, not even bothering to look up.

"Not much," I say, figuring the less said the better. "Why do you think he's going there?"

"Why? To ruin his life, that's why," Fred says, and I have to admit I do feel pretty sorry for the guy. I mean, look at his family: Shirley's a useless housewife who doesn't even cook or clean; Mike's a total pothead on his way to Honolulu; and he doesn't know it yet, but his only daughter's about to become a high school dropout.

✖ ✖ ✖

The next day I'm upstairs in my room just minding my own business when Fred calls me into the kitchen.

"Let's go," he says, like he's in a big hurry.

"Where?"

"For your first driving lesson. C'mon, get your coat on."

"Go on, Andrea," Shirley says. "Your father's doing you a favor. Don't keep him waiting."

"Just a second," I say, turning to go back upstairs. "I have to get my learner's permit." To tell you the truth, I'm not thrilled with the idea of Fred teaching me what to do behind the wheel or with the idea of driving in general, and if I weren't taking off with Frank, I wouldn't have even bothered to get my permit. I know that sounds shocking, since that's what every kid on Long Island lives for: to have a set of wheels. Like Donald Caruso, who finally got his license after failing the test twice and now drives his mother's car around, honking his head off so everyone will notice. I mean, big deal, any idiot can learn to drive.

"Go get in the car," Fred says when I come back into the kitchen. "I'll be out in a minute."

Normally I would say something like *Sure, I have to hurry up just so I can wait for you,* but I hold my tongue, say good-bye to Shirley, and step outside. I'm a little nervous getting into the car by myself but I take a deep breath, open the door, and slide behind the wheel. And even though I have my key, I don't put it into the ignition until Fred is sitting beside me.

"Ladies, start your engines," he announces, which is supposed to be funny though I don't know why. I start the car and Fred says, "Don't be afraid to give her some gas," so after I make sure we're still in park, I do. Fred shows me how to work the windshield wipers, the lights, the turn signals, and the horn, and I try them all. So far so good, though of course we haven't moved two inches yet.

"Now put her in reverse, and slowly back out of the driveway," Fred instructs me. I do as I'm told, but before we get even three feet, Fred yanks on my hair. "Whoa, Nellie," he says. "You're going way too fast."

I brake, and Fred and I both lurch forward. Fred sighs and shakes his head. "Try not to slam on the brakes like that."

"Sorry."

"Try it again," he says, and this time I do a lot better. I get to the end of the driveway and stop smoothly before I pull into the road. At the corner, I brake at the stop sign and wait for Fred to tell me what to do.

"Turn right," he says, "and be careful you don't swerve out to the left like your brother."

I take the turn and keep driving. "Wait a minute," Fred says, unbuckling his seat belt. "I don't think your side-view mirror is adjusted right." He slides over until he's sitting right next to me and reaches across my lap to roll down my window.

"I'll do it." I open the window and fix the mirror. Fred leans back as I take the right, but two seconds later, he's leaning forward again, practically sitting on top of me.

"You forgot to put your signal on." His arm shoots out to demonstrate. "This lever here, to the left of the steering wheel, is your turn signal. It goes down to signal left and up to signal right."

"I know, I know. I'm not a moron," I say, and I brake so hard we both go flying again.

"Don't be so heavy-footed with the brake," Fred says, putting his hand on my knee. "Lighten up on the pedal. Try not to—"

"Move over!" I yell. "Don't sit so close to me!"

"What?" Fred tilts his head to the side, wearing this baffled expression like all of a sudden he's lost command of the English language. And though he takes his hand off my leg, he doesn't move an inch.

"Move over!" I yell again. "God, I'm so sick of you always being right in my face! I can hardly *breathe,* Fred. Give me some *room.*"

"What? What is the matter with you?" Fred stares at me with this shocked look in his eyes, like I might be having a brain seizure. "I was only trying to—"

"Don't whine," I say in a cold, Franklike tone of voice, which startles and pleases me at the same time. "Just move over," I tell him, my voice low and steady. "Now."

Fred is too stunned to respond, so he just studies me like he can't believe what I just said. I stare him down until he finally slides back across the seat and buckles up again. I throw him one more "I mean business" look and then drive us through the neighborhood. We don't say another word until we pull back into our driveway.

"You did pretty well for your first time," Fred says as I put the car in park. "You're going to be an excellent driver."

"Yeah, whatever." I pull the key out of the ignition.

"You just need practice," he says. "Another year and you'll have your license. . . ." His voice trails off. "It's amazing how time flies, isn't it? It seems like it was just yesterday I was changing your diapers. . . ."

The thought of that really creeps me out. "I'm not your little girl anymore," I say in a low voice.

"I know that," Fred says.

"Well, then act like you know it." Suddenly I'm furious again. "I'm a grown woman, okay? I've got my own life. I am not your personal property." He cringes as my voice rises. "I don't have to wait on you hand and foot, I don't have to cook your disgusting dinners, and I don't have to go out with you for ice cream or anything else." I fling open the car door and storm into the house, slamming the front door behind me.

Shirley's in the kitchen, talking to someone on the phone. "Mike? How is he?" she says into the receiver, like she's thinking it over. "Oh, he's fine. Fine. He's off skiing with some of his college friends, doesn't that sound like fun? He'll probably be home sometime next week."

Leave it to Shirley to keep the charade going. Oh yeah, fine, fine. We're just one big happy family.

"Hold on a second," I hear her say. "Andrea, is that you? Is everything okay?"

"Peachy keen," I say. "Jim dandy." Then I run up the stairs and slam my bedroom door.

The rest of the week passes slowly, but then almost before I know it, it's Sunday, the day before I'm leaving with Frank. I'm not sure what to bring with me and I can't take much; it's not like I can pack a suitcase—*that* would be real subtle—but I can put some stuff in my knapsack. If I leave my books home there's a lot of room in it, and I can just tell my teachers I forgot them and look on with someone else.

I guess I should pack some clothes, you know, a sweater or two and some pants. I open my dresser drawers and pick out a few things. It's hot in the south, so I'll probably have to buy all new clothes anyway. I think I should take the things that are important to me, so I open my jewelry box and take out my gold name necklace, the Jewish star my grandmother gave me, and the leather bracelet from Ronnie. And my birthday locket, of course. And I think I'll bring some photos since they don't take up much room. Here's one of Mike and me building a snowman when I was little, and here's another of Fred and Shirley all dressed up to go to a wedding. And I think I'll take the picture of my sister Melissa that I stole from Shirley's box of photos too.

What else do I want? I look around my room, and my eyes fall on my bed. And even though it's incredibly babyish to take a stuffed animal along, I stuff Snowball into my knapsack. "You'll be okay," I tell her, tucking her head inside. I wish I could take some of my books with me: *Winnie-the-Pooh* and the endangered-animal book I got from Mike for my birthday, but I don't have room. I guess eventually Shirley can mail my stuff to wherever I am.

When I'm done packing, I reach into my pocket for my money, drag it out, and count it up. I have what's left of my birthday loot and a few twenties I took from Shirley's purse, which comes to two hundred ten dollars total. That should get us pretty far, I guess. And Frank will have some money too.

I really want to leave a note for the Rental Units, but I'm sure Frank would kill me if I did something stupid like that. I don't even know what I'd say. *So long, suckers?* I mean, it's weird, because I don't even like my parents very much, but in a way I think I'm going to miss them.

Well, I'm all packed up and ready to go. The last thing I have to do is go downstairs and say good night to the Units. They're sitting in the living room, and for once in my life, I don't make a big deal of walking through all their smoke.

"Good night, Fred. Good night Shirley," I say, standing a little away from the couch. Ever since my outburst in the car I've kept my distance from Fred and vice versa.

"Bedtime?" Shirley asks. "Too bad you have to go back to school tomorrow, Andrea. It's been nice having you around."

I'm tempted to go over and feel Shirley's forehead to see if she has a fever because she has never, and I repeat, *never,* said anything like this before. I didn't even know she cared.

"Well, you could let me stay home if that's the way you feel about it," I say, knowing she never would.

"Soon you'll be off to college and the house will be so lonely," Shirley says. I guess she's starting to get the empty nest syndrome on account of Mike being so far away. Too bad I can't tell her the house will be lonely much sooner than she thinks.

After I say goodnight to Fred and Shirley, I go back up to my room and get ready for bed. I doubt I'll be able to sleep at all, but I have to try because tomorrow's a very big day. First I have to get through school, which seems totally impossible, and then I have to walk to the fence, say good-bye to Bessie if she's out, jump in the car with Frank, and go. And we'll probably stay up all night because we have to drive as far as possible to keep the cops off our trail. I wonder how long it will take Shirley and Fred to figure out I'm missing in action. And when they do, I wonder if they'll come after me or leave me alone so I can "ruin my life" just like Mike.

I snuggle down under my blankets (for the last time!), but before I shut my eyes, I actually pinch myself to make sure I'm not dreaming, because if you really stop to think about it, this is almost too good to be true.

EIGHTEEN

The first day of school after vacation is nothing but a major waste of time. Instead of paying attention in class, everyone's blabbing about what they got for Christmas or Chanukah, showing off their tans if they happened to be lucky enough to go somewhere warm over the holidays, or bragging about how drunk they got on New Year's Eve. I couldn't care less except for one very interesting tidbit of gossip: it seems Donna Rizzo actually came to her senses and dumped Donald Caruso over vacation. See, Donna went away with her family to some Caribbean island for Christmas, and while they were there, she met a college guy and let him go to third base with her, or maybe even further, depending on who you get the story from. But it's definitely true because I saw Donna in the cafeteria with my own eyes and she was wearing a gigantic college ring on a chain around her neck and looking all moony besides. So now Donald is the laughingstock of our school because Donna never let him lay a hand on her. Poor Donald. My heart really bleeds for him, let me tell you.

What I should really do is go up to Donna Rizzo and personally thank her, because if Donald didn't have his own problems, I'm sure he'd be shooting off his mouth about seeing me and Frank on the side of the road the day we hit the squirrel right before vacation. But Donald's got other things on his puny mind right now, which is a lucky break for me. I wouldn't be surprised if he's forgotten all about it.

After school, I race to my spot by the fence to wait for Frank, but guess what. He's not there. I can't believe he's late today of all days, the day we're hitting the road. For God's sake, what in the world is wrong with him? I made sure I was here on time, so you'd think he could at least do the same. But nope, there's nothing here but me, a fence, an empty pasture, and a sky full of gray clouds that better not open up and dump a load of snow on my head while I'm standing here freezing to death.

Simmer, Andi, I tell myself, taking a few deep breaths to calm my nerves. I'm sure Frank will be here any minute. He'll probably tell me he wanted to give me a little more time just in case I changed my mind, like he did on my birthday. But still, it's so cold out here I can see my breath, and besides, you'd think the guy would know how hyped up I am to go away with him, so where is he already?

To try and keep warm, I start pacing, and then I start walking around in little circles, just like my mind is going around in circles. God, what if something happened to Frank? What if he got into an accident or something? How would I find out? Frank doesn't know my phone number or even my real name so how would he ever find me? And I don't know how to find him either. I don't know his last name; I don't know where he lives. I don't know anything about him, really, except he has a friend named Lloyd, like that's a big help. I mean, what if something terrible happened? What if Frank's lying on the side of the road somewhere, bleeding to death, and when the ambulance comes, he says, *Tell Vanessa I love her,* and then he dies before the ambulance driver can even say, *Vanessa who?*

God, I'm such a worrywart. I've got the guy dead and buried already and he's only a few minutes late. I'm sure he's okay. Frank's a good driver, so I doubt he had an accident. Maybe the car broke down. That's a definite possibility since the Volkswagen isn't exactly in mint condition.

While I'm thinking all this, I hear a car come up the road, so I snap my head around, but it's just some housewife with curlers in her hair driving a station wagon. I look down quickly, because I don't want anyone to see my face in case they put my picture in the paper when the Rents realize I'm missing. One of the first things I'll have to do when we get out of here is come up with a disguise. I'll probably have to cut my hair, which won't make Frank happy. But we'll both have to make sacrifices.

Maybe Frank has the flu. Maybe he's lying in bed somewhere with a runny nose and a temperature, totally bummed out that we can't leave today. There's some kind of flu going around; lots of kids were absent today, though I bet some of them were still away on vacation.

"Okay, Andrea Robin." I stop pacing and start talking to myself. "Obviously something's come up but Frank had no way of telling you. I'm sure he'll be here right on time tomorrow with a perfectly good explanation about why he couldn't come today. And I bet he'd get really mad if he could hear all the thoughts racing around in your head because then he'd think you don't trust him. And of course you trust him. You wouldn't be stupid enough to run away with a guy you didn't trust, would you?" The question, along with my white puffs of breath, hangs in the air.

✖ ✖ ✖

Frank didn't show up on Tuesday, Wednesday, or Thursday either. Now it's Friday, and if he doesn't come today, I don't know what I'll do. I'm so upset I can hardly think, and I have to lean against the fence post because my legs feel all shaky, they really do. Plus I have this sick feeling in my stomach that I'm never going to see Frank again and I just can't figure out why. I mean, what did I do? That last day we were together was so totally perfect.

What could have happened? Maybe Frank's the one who needed eleven days apart so he could think things over, and after he did, maybe he decided he didn't want to go through with it. But why? And wouldn't he at least come by to tell me? He knows I'm standing out here freezing my jugs off. Not showing up for a whole lousy week is just so completely *rude*.

I close my eyes and squeeze them tight because I really don't want to cry, and anyway, it's so cold my tears would probably freeze and wouldn't I look like an idiot with icicles hanging from my eyeballs when Frank shows up? He has to show today, he just has to. *Please, please, please, let me hear the sound of a car slowing down,* I pray to whoever up there might hear me. *Please.*

And then, believe it or not, one second later I do hear a car. It doesn't sound like Frank's car, but it's been so long, maybe I don't recognize the Volkswagen anymore. I keep my eyes closed because if it isn't Frank, I don't want to know who it is. The car stops a little ahead of me and before I can open my eyes, I hear a familiar voice say, "Hey, Dee-Dee, what are you doing, meditating?"

Just my luck. There's only one person in the world who can sound so stupid: Donald Caruso. He's actually parked his car and is standing beside it with his arms folded, leaning against the trunk. I keep my eyes closed, trying to heed the words of wisdom Shirley bestowed upon me one time when a horsefly was bothering me at the beach: "Just ignore it, Andrea, and it'll go away." But of course it didn't; it bit me, in fact, and guess what—Donald Caruso isn't going away either.

"So, what's up, Dee-Dee?" he calls, like all of a sudden we're best friends. I don't answer him, but instead of getting back in his car and driving off, he comes over to me.

"What do you want?" I ask him in an "I'm not in the mood for any of your BS" tone.

"Nothing. Can't a guy just say hello?"

I look at him like he's lost his mind. Why in the world would Donald Caruso want to say hello to me?

"Isn't it a *dee*-lightful day?" Donald asks, leaning against the fence and tilting his head up toward the sun. "So, Dee-Dee, heard anything from your *girlfriend* lately?"

"Donald, why do you keep asking me that?" I say, not in a nasty voice, but like I really want to know. "I mean, do you get off on thinking that I'm a lesbian or what? Like do you imagine me and Ronnie doing it to turn yourself on, or—"

"Shut up, Dee-Dee, okay?" He pushes himself off the fence and starts walking back toward his car without looking at me.

"Maybe you're the lezzie, Donald," I call after him, which is totally stupid since everyone knows you can't be a lesbian unless you're a girl. "Maybe you're the homo, Donald." I start walking toward him, really yelling now. "Maybe that's why Donna needed to find herself a new boyfriend. I bet you couldn't even get it up."

Donald turns and glares at me. "Just shut up about Donna, Dee-Dee. I mean it. Shut up or else I'll—"

"You'll what?"

Donald spins around and wraps his arms around

himself. Then he moves his hands up and down, caressing his own shoulders and neck so that from the back it looks like someone's making out with him. "Oh, Dee-Dee! Oh, baby . . ." He moans and smacks his lips together loudly and then stops to turn and face me. "I'll call your mother and tell her about your boyfriend."

"Go ahead," I say, like I couldn't care less.

"Or maybe I'll call your dad," Donald says. "Yeah, that's what I'll do. Hello, Dr. Kaplan?" Donald puts his fist up to his ear like he's talking on the phone. "How are you? Do you know your ugly daughter's been seeing some older guy who drives a brown Volkswagen after school? How do I know? I saw them by the side of the road a few days before Christmas vacation. And believe me, they looked awfully cozy."

"You wouldn't dare tell my father about me and Frank," I say, my voice barely a whisper.

"Frank! Thanks for telling me his name, Dee-Dee. Yes, Dr. Kaplan, his name is Frank. Frank . . . what did you say his last name was?"

"None of your business," I tell Donald.

"Frank None-of-Your-Business, Dr. Kaplan." Donald slowly lowers his hand and grins, knowing that he's got me.

"Donald," I say, "listen, this is serious. You can't tell my father about me and Frank. I mean it." This is awful. If—no, *when* Frank shows up to take me away from all this, he's going to totally kill me because now Donald knows his name and what kind of car he drives and that'll spoil everything.

"Please, Donald." I toss my pride out the window and beg the guy. "Pretty please, with sugar on top."

"Yeah, yeah, yeah. Blow me," Donald says, yanking open his car door.

"Okay," I say, like it's no big deal.

"Wha-a-at?" He freezes, all bent over, half in and half out of the car.

"I said okay. You said blow me, and I said okay. I'll do what you want if you do what I want: keep your big mouth shut about me and Frank. Deal?"

"Where?" This time Donald's voice is barely a whisper.

"Get in," I say, going around to the other side of the car. I throw my knapsack in and jump in after it. Donald starts the motor, but before he can even put the car into drive, I put my hand on his crotch.

"Shouldn't we go somewhere?" Donald asks, his voice all breathy.

"Just shut the car off," I say, and he does. I mean, why not? There's plenty of room in here: the front seat of Donald's mother's car is huge, compared to Frank's, anyway.

"Just relax now, Donald," I say. "I won't hurt you. C'mon, let me see what you've got in there."

Donald hitches up his hips, undoes his fly and pulls his pants and underwear down to his knees.

"Just lean back and shut your eyes," I say in a soothing voice. Donald does as he's told and I reach over and take him gently in my hands. He lets out a huge sigh and reaches his arm across my back to push me down toward his lap. When my head is about two inches from his crotch, I twist my wrists hard and fast in opposite directions, like his penis is a sopping wet washcloth that needs to be wrung out.

"Ow!" Donald's voice goes up an entire octave, his whole body jerks, and his eyes snap open. "What are you, crazy, Dee-Dee? Man, that hurt! What are you trying to do, pull it off? I thought you were going to blow me."

"Yeah, right." I laugh. "You really thought I would put that microscopic peanut in my—"

"Shut up, you—" Donald lunges toward me but I stop him by reaching into my pocket, pulling out my Swiss army knife, and snapping it open.

"Hey, hey, what the . . . ?" All of a sudden Donald realizes how exposed he is and his hands fly to his lap to cover himself. "Dee-Dee," he says, "put that thing away. Please? C'mon now, I'm sorry. Let's just forget this ever happened, all right?"

"No way," I say, looking him right in the eye. "Now you listen to me, you stupid jock." I lay my hand flat on the seat between us. "You better not say a word about this and you better stop calling me Dee-Dee, you understand? Because if I can do this to myself"—I inhale sharply and run the blade right across the tip of my pinkie—"believe me, I could do a whole lot worse to you." And then, just to make sure he gets my point, I slice the tip of my finger a few more times.

"Hey, c'mon, cut it out. Quit it." Donald is totally pale, like all the blood spilling from my pinkie is draining out of his face. For a split second, I feel totally peaceful, and I think, *Frank, you should have told me, it doesn't hurt at all,* but then the pain explodes all the way up my arm and I feel light-headed and nauseous and I start breathing really fast. The only way to stop the pain is to keep cutting myself, so I do, until Donald reaches over and grabs the knife out of my hand.

"For cryin' out loud, Dee-Dee—I mean, Andi." Donald quickly corrects himself. "What are you, nuts? Look what you're doing to my mother's car." Donald pulls himself together and starts searching for something to wipe up the blood with.

"Your concern is so . . . so touching," I say, making a fist around my pinkie with my other hand and squeezing it tight to stop the bleeding.

"What are you, really losing it, Andi? What are you trying to do, kill yourself? And look at this mess. What am I supposed to tell my mother?"

"Tell her you got your period," I say, and then I start laughing hysterically like a total lunatic.

Donald gives me a funny look and leans over the seat and tries to mop up the blood with the hem of his T-shirt because he can't think of what else to do. And neither can I, so I grab my knapsack, get out of the car, and head home, keeping my hand way up in the air because that's what we learned in health class, to elevate a wound high over your heart, if you have one. And then when I get home, I fix up my finger myself, even though it's cut pretty bad and I should probably go to the emergency room and show it to someone and get a tetanus shot or maybe some stitches or something. But I don't care. In fact, I don't ever want my pinkie to heal. Or if it does heal, I want it to leave a huge, jagged, bumpy, ugly scar so that for the rest of my life, whenever I look down at it, I'll always, always remember.

Epilogue

All right, all right, since I'm sure you're just dying to know, first of all, no, I didn't get gangrene and my pinkie didn't fall off. After I got home and doctored it up, I avoided Shirley until suppertime. When she finally spotted my Band-Aid, I told her I cut my finger on a can of peas I was opening to serve Fred and it was no big deal. On Monday I showed it to the school nurse, who said it was just a superficial wound, which surprised me since there was so much blood and everything. My finger does have a wicked scar on it, though, which will probably be there for life.

Second of all, you'll be happy to know that Donald

Caruso had a major personality change after our little encounter in his mother's car and treats me quite nicely now. I think he's pretty scared of me because whenever I see him in the hall at school, he always goes out of his way to say "Hi, Andi" nice and loud, and he's even stopped teasing me with all the lezzie stuff, which is a big relief.

And third of all, just in case you're wondering, no, Frank never came back. And I've been thinking about him a lot today, December 17, 1972, which just happens to be my seventeenth birthday.

"Aren't you going to wish me a happy birthday?" I ask Bessie, who's busy eating a fistful of grass out of my hand. It's an unusually warm day for December, and old Bessie's out in her field today, which is like a birthday present to me because she's still better company than 99 percent of the people I know. While she chews, I tell her my unexciting birthday plans: first my family will eat dinner made by Shirley, who will cook something for the first time since last December, since it's a special occasion, and then we'll have the usual celebration with the same old chocolate cake with white and yellow frosting. And Shirley, Fred, and Mike will all sing "Happy Birthday" in their same old off-key voices and give me presents, and my grandmother will send me a corny card with some loot tucked inside.

Mike, for your information, is back living at home. He never even made it to Hawaii, which is typical. He got as far as San Francisco and hung out there for a while with a bunch of hippies he met at a bookstore called City

Lights that specializes in beat poetry. But then his money ran out, and I don't know, I guess he found out that life on the road is more glamorous when you read about it in a book by Jack Kerouac than when you actually live it.

Mike isn't too happy being back home, let me tell you. He's working at a bookstore in the mall and—get this—the Rents are actually making him pay for room and board. Fred thinks hitting him in the wallet will teach Mike something about being a responsible adult, but I have serious doubts about that.

Anyway, I'm glad Mike's around because now I have someone to talk to. I even told him about me and Frank, more or less.

It was one of those rare days when Mike was laying off the weed, and we were hanging out in his room. Mike was sprawled across his beanbag chair and I was lying on his bed, both of us staring at the blobs moving up and down in the Lava lamp on his dresser.

"So," Mike said, "what ever happened to that guy Frankenstein you told me about last year on your birthday?"

"Nothing happened to him," I said, but Mike pressed me, so I told him the whole story. Well, not the whole story—there are some gory details that are way too embarrassing for a baby sister to tell her big brother—but I told him enough so he got the picture. The whole time I was talking, Mike was staring down at his hands, and then when I was done, he stayed quiet for a minute. I was scared he was going to be angry or, I don't know, disgusted with me or something, but when he raised his eyes, they looked so soft and tender, and *concerned*, that a big lump formed in my throat and I almost couldn't breathe.

"Oh, Squirt," Mike said, his voice gentle, "don't you know you deserve to be treated better than that?"

I thought for a second, then shrugged. "I don't know. I guess."

"You guess? I'm sorry, Squirt." Mike sounded so sad I thought he might cry.

"Sorry for what? You didn't do anything."

"Exactly," Mike said. "I didn't protect you. That's *my* sister," he said, pointing to himself and speaking in a tough-guy voice. "You can look but you better not touch."

"Oh, Mike," I said, and then before I could stop myself, I started to blubber. Mike came over to the bed and took me in his arms and held me and rocked me and told me that everything was going to be okay. I cried for a long time and when I finally stopped, Mike said if Frank ever dared show his ugly face in this town again, it would resemble a bowl of chopped liver before he got through with it. That made me laugh, since Mike's not exactly the fighting type. But then he got all serious.

"Listen, Squirt," he said. "Just because a guy has the hots for you doesn't mean he loves you, you know what I'm saying?"

"Yeah." I nodded. "I guess I was pretty stupid, wasn't I?"

"It's not your fault," Mike said, smoothing a piece of hair behind my ear. "That moron"—Mike almost spat—"really took advantage of you."

"But I *let* him take advantage of me," I said, my voice all shaky like I might cry again.

"Squirt, don't blame yourself." Mike hugged me close. "He was the adult and you were the kid. You didn't know any better. And it's not like either of us learned how to have a normal relationship by watching the people around here." He jerked his head toward Fred and Shirley's bedroom. "You'll do better next time, Squirt. Just remember you're an important person, okay?"

"I am?" I whispered.

"Of course you are. You're important to me. Why do you think I came home? To hang out with the Rents?"

"Not bloody likely," I say in a fake British accent, which makes us both laugh.

"I guess I wasn't the sharpest knife in the drawer, was I, Bessie?" I ask, giving her another handful of grass to munch. While she's thinking it over, a car pulls up right by the fence post where Frank used to pick me up. Oh my God, I can't believe it. Can it possibly be Frank? The car isn't a Volkswagen—I think it's some kind of Ford—but still, my heart starts beating a million times a minute and I break into a sweat. What if it is Frank? What would I say to him?

"Would he really remember my birthday?" I ask Bessie, my voice barely a whisper. I either have to turn around right now and get the heck out of here or walk right past the car to see whether it's Frank or not, and to tell you the truth, I'm not sure what I want to do. The smart part of me thinks if I never see Frank's face again, it'll be too soon, but there's another part of me, too. A part that wants to march right over there and give him a piece of my mind. *Why don't you go pick on someone your own size?* I want to yell at him, though that probably isn't such a great idea because when Frank gets mad, there's no telling what might happen.

While I'm trying to figure out what I'm going to do, my legs start moving and my feet keep putting themselves down one in front of the other, so I guess my body isn't going to wait for my head to decide.

"Vanessa." My stomach lurches at the sound of my old name, and I stop dead in my tracks. "C'mere, Vanessa. I've got something for you."

I know I shouldn't go anywhere near that car, but my body just floats over to it like I'm walking in my sleep.

"Hey, Frank," I say, but then I feel like an idiot, because this guy isn't Frank. His hair is curlier and lighter, and he's got freckles, too. I don't know whether I'm relieved or disappointed. Mostly just surprised, I guess. How does this guy know who I am?

"Vanessa," he says again, like he's trying my name on for size. "Vanessa, honey, I'm Lloyd, Frank's sidekick, and I sure am glad to meet you. You're ten times prettier than those pictures—I mean, than Frank said you were."

My face turns beet red and I almost spit, I'm so mad. I can't believe Frank showed Lloyd the pictures he took of me, after he said he wouldn't. *Don't you trust me, Vanessa?* I swear, I could just vomit.

"Well, yeah, I saw them, Vanessa. Frank was so proud, he couldn't help showing you off a little. And you can't blame him really—I mean, look at you. His photos didn't come close to doing you justice." Lloyd gives a low whistle. "You really are drop-dead gorgeous."

Yeah, right, I think, *and your prick is the size of Alaska.*

"I mean, Frank said you were a real doll, but—"

"Where is he?" I blurt out in the middle of Lloyd's BS.

"Frank? Who knows?" Lloyd shrugs. "Frank's like the wind, honey. He blows in and out of town whenever he feels like it. He could be right around the corner, he could be a thousand miles away. But never mind Frank, Vanessa. Good-bye and good riddance."

"You're telling me."

"Hey, hey, don't be so hard on the guy." For some reason, now that I agree with him, Lloyd changes his tune. "Frank does have a heart, Vanessa. Look, he asked me to give you this." Lloyd holds out a small white envelope and I take it in my hand.

For a minute I look at what I'm holding like I don't know what to do with it, but then Lloyd says, "Open it," so I do. Inside is a piece of paper ripped from a notebook. I unfold it and read, *Dear Vanessa. Happy birthday and congratulations. You're not jailbait anymore. Frank.* And taped to the bottom is my mother's wedding ring.

I can't believe Frank actually did something nice for a change. *Maybe he isn't such a bad guy after all,* I think, and then, as if he can read my mind, Lloyd sets me straight.

"Don't get any ideas that Frank's turned into a saint, Vanessa," he says, and every time he says my name—or what he thinks is my name—he says it with a hiss, *Vanessssa,* like he's letting all the air out of a bicycle tire.

"This was all my idea. When I heard Frank had your mother's wedding ring, I was appalled, honey, I really was. He was going to pawn it, for God's sake, but I challenged him to a poker game and managed to win it back for you. And that was no small feat because Frank is a real cardsharp, let me tell you. But enough about Frank." Lloyd waves his hand like he's shooing away a fly. "Why don't you get in the car and I'll give you a ride?"

I stand stock-still and ponder Lloyd's offer while he keeps talking; I can tell he's the kind of guy who just loves the sound of his own voice. "You don't have to worry about me, Vanessa," he says. "I'm a perfect gentleman. Not all guys are louses like Frank, you know. I'll take you right home, or anywhere else you want to go. Like, how about we swing into Manhattan? I know all the good places. We could have a nice dinner, see a show, go to a club, whatever you want. Me and you could have a real nice time together, doll. What do you think?"

I think Long Island is chock-full of perverts, no matter how serene and safe Shirley and Fred say it is. That's what I think. But I don't tell Lloyd that. I just walk around to the passenger side of the car without a word. Before I even get there, Lloyd reaches over to unlock the door and push it open, to show me he's a perfect gentleman, just like he said. But instead of getting into the car, I hop the fence, run my hand along Bessie's back as I walk by her, and cut across her pasture.

"Hey!" Lloyd calls out. "Hey, Vanessa. Where are you going?"

Home, I turn around and mouth to him. Where there's

at least one person who knows I'm important. I mean, what does Lloyd think, I'm still as stupid as I look?

"Vanessa, come back," Lloyd calls. "Vanessa? Vanessa!"

That's my name, don't wear it out, I think, and then I correct myself: That isn't my name. My name is Andi. With an *i*. Short for Andrea. Andrea Robin Kaplan. That's what people call me now. *If* they want me to answer.